Pink Cad

Todd Strasser

Pink Cadillac

Based on a screenplay by
John Eskow

Pan Original   Pan Books
London, Sydney and Auckland

First published in Great Britain by Pan Books Ltd,
Cavaye Place, London SW10 9PG
by arrangement with New American Library
a division of Penguin Books USA Inc.

9 8 7 6 5 4 3 2 1
Novelization by Todd Strasser based
on a screenplay by John Eskow
© Warner Brothers 1989
ISBN 0 330 31245 6

Printed in Great Britain by,
Richard Clay Ltd, Bungay, Suffolk

1

The battered black Plymouth Fury roared out of the saw-toothed Tehachpi Mountains and hit the Mojave doing seventy-five. Inside, Tommy Nowak drove with his left foot on the gas and his right leg stretched out on the seat beside him, the tip of his alligator cowboy boot practically touching the passenger door. He'd covered more than 300 miles in just over four hours, stopping only once for coffee, a couple of Twinkies and a fresh tank of gas.

Tommy shifted in the seat, tucked his leg in and stretched a muscular arm between the head-rests. Finding unusual positions to drive in was nothing new for him. When you covered as many miles a year as he did, you either came up with some pretty creative ways of sitting or you got awful sore. It was not uncommon for him to do 100,000 miles a year, sometimes more. The Fury's odometer had rolled over six times before sticking permanently at 000001.

He pulled a Marlboro out of his T-shirt and lit it with the car's lighter – just about the only device in the dashboard that still worked. He took a deep drag and held the smoke in his lungs to absorb that first satisfying nicotine fix. He'd been on the road for five days, averaging roughly four hours of sleep a night, and he was starting to feel a bit singed.

Outside, the Mojave, with its rocky dryness, tall Saguaro cactus, ghost towns and dry salt lakes quickly passed by. Tommy exhaled his first drag slowly. This was the land of tumbleweed and sidewinders, the land of the good, the bad and the ugly, where a man was especially free to indulge in life, liberty and, in Tommy's case, the pursuit of fugitives from justice, otherwise known as skips.

Tommy was a professional fugitive hunter, or skip chaser. He was hired by bail bondsmen when men accused of serious crimes skipped their court appearances and became fugitives, thus putting their often substantial bail bonds in jeopardy of being forfeited. Tommy had pursued his craft for nearly twenty years with a single-minded determination that made him something of a legend. He was a loner who could be counted on to help out another skip chaser in a pinch, a hard man who was none the less infuriated by injustice. In his time only three fugitives had eluded his capture. One went to Cuba, which was outside Tommy's jurisdiction; one disappeared without a trace in the Canadian Rockies; the third had a sex-change operation and joined an order of nuns who helped the poor in Central America. Tommy could have apprehended that last skip, but he figured anyone who wanted their freedom *that* badly probably deserved it.

In the car, he shifted his lean, hard body again, still searching for a comfortable position. Part of the problem was the interior of the Fury, which had been designed before the word ergonomics gained popular usage. But mostly it was just that antsy feeling that always came over him when he knew he was closing in on a skip.

It was around four in the afternoon when Tommy reached Rustville, a microdot in the desert whose reason for being had long since been forgotten. He pulled up in front of the police station, located in a Quonset hut that looked like a very large, dirty green oil drum lying on its side and half submerged in the ground. There were two windows and a door on each end, with a stovepipe and a large antenna poking out of the roof.

Tommy got out of the Fury and stretched. He gazed around at the barren and burning expanses of desert and the heaped masses of the San Bernardino Mountains in the background, then reached into the front seat and scooped up a couple of tapes. From the trunk he took out a black drum box on casters in which he carried the supplies he'd need to convince the skip that this was his lucky day. Thus equipped, he entered the Quonset hut.

Tommy had been in plenty of police stations in his life, on both friendly and some not so friendly terms, but he could not recall a station so dingy, run-down and utterly stripped of dignity. Inside, a beefy sergeant lounged behind the booking desk ruminating over a beef jerky, and a young patrolman was slumped in a wooden chair. Both were watching Oprah on a small television mounted on the wall next to five dented metal lockers. An oscillating fan on the booking desk rotated back and forth, alternately ruffling the sergeant's sparce hair and the pages of a desk calendar. To Tommy the place looked as if it hadn't seen a criminal in twenty years.

The officers glanced with little curiosity at Tommy, who'd neglected to shave for several days and was wearing jeans, a black T-shirt and a John Deere cap. They probably figured he was just another trucker who'd come by to ask directions or complain that some hooker had slipped him a mickey in a motel the previous night and stolen his wallet.

'What's she got today?' Tommy asked, glancing at the screen at the newly slimmed talk show host who'd lost weight so quickly it seemed as if she'd unzipped her old body one day and stepped out sixty pounds thinner.

'Another bunch of transsexuals,' the sergeant said, gesturing at the two women and one man on the screen. 'Griping about how hard it is to find a date.'

'You know what Woody Allen used to say,' Tommy said.

'No, what?' asked the patrolman.

'Best thing to be is bisexual. Then you got twice as much chance on Saturday night.'

'Sounds reasonable,' said the sergeant. 'Now who the hell's Woody Allen?'

'Don't he make movies?' the patrolman asked. 'Come on, Sarge, ain't you ever seen *Bananas*?'

'Every time I go to the supermarket.'

'What about *Annie Hall*?'

'That hooker still in town? I thought she moved over to Needles.'

'Hey, listen,' Tommy said. 'I hate to interrupt the film class, but is Ed Flynn around?'

'Who's askin'?' asked the sergeant.

'Tom Nowak.'

The young patrolman straightened up. 'The skip tracer?'

Tommy nodded.

'Wow, Ed's told us all about you,' the patrolman gushed. 'I was about ready to believe you was nothin' but a figment of his imagination.'

'Ed's in the back,' the sergeant said, heaving himself up. 'I'll go get him.'

Tommy took a Marlboro out of his shirt and lit it. The chief of police in Rustville was a fellow named Ed Flynn, who Tommy had met in a military hospital back in Viet Nam. Tommy had had about thirty small pieces of US military shrapnel taken out of his back after some dimwit radioed the wrong co-ordinates to the artillery. Ed had taken a single shot in the right thigh that had fractured the femur and left him with a permanent limp. They eventually shipped home together and would up in California, staying in touch as they pursued a variety of careers loosely related to the field of law enforcement.

'It true about you gettin' dressed up as a rodeo clown to get that bull rider?' the patrolman asked.

Tommy nodded.

'How the hell'd you do it?'

'Just grabbed him, that's all.'

'There he is!' Tommy turned and saw Flynn come out of the back, limping, his police chief's shirt unbuttoned almost down to his protruding navel. He looked like he'd put on weight and it seemed to make the limp more pronounced. They shook hands.

'How the hell are you, Tommy?' Flynn asked, smiling.

'Can't complain, Ed. You?'

'Nothin' a double Scotch on the rocks can't cure,' Flynn said, pulling a bottle out from behind the booking desk. 'One for you?'

'Make it a single,' Tommy said. 'I'm still working. By the way, you didn't forget that limo, did ya?'

'Hell no,' said Flynn. 'She's on her way from San Bernardino right now. Don't have much call for limos around here, you understand. Now go on, tell 'em about Capshaw.'

'I told him,' Tommy said.

'The hell you did,' Flynn said, opening a small refrigerator against the wall and cracking some ice out of a plastic tray. 'They wanted this boy Capshaw for grand larceny up in Stockton and he skipped on a pretty big bond. What was it, Tommy? Ten? Fifteen?'

'Twenty-five,' Tommy said.

'Right.' Ed dropped the ice into a couple of rock glasses. 'So Buddy Donovan was the bondsman and he must've sent three bounty hunters after him. Capshaw was about six foot six and ran two-fifty, maybe two-sixty. The first two hunters couldn't find him and the third wound up in the hospital with concussion and three broken ribs, so old Buddy finally asks Tommy here.'

'How come he didn't ask you first?' the sergeant asked.

Tommy smiled. 'Well, let's just say I'm the skip tracer of the last resort.'

'They don't use Tommy unless they have to,' Ed said, handing Tommy his drink. 'Anyway, Capshaw liked to ride bulls and they knew he was gonna be at the rodeo up in Fresno, so Tommy calls me up and says why don't we meet there for a drink 'cause it's half-way between his place and mine, and he figures he might need a little help with Capshaw if things get tight.'

'Hell I did,' Tommy smirked.

'Yeah, well, I get up there to the fair grounds and here comes Tommy in a goddamn clown suit. I mean, with one of them red bulb noses and this red Bozo hair and his shirt all polka-dotted. So I say, "Now what the hell're you gonna do in that?" and Tommy says, "Just watch."'

'How the hell'd you know anything about rodeo clowning anyway?' the patrolman asked.

'Hell, he's been a clown all his life,' Flynn laughed, nudging Tommy with his elbow. 'So anyway, the bull riding begins and pretty soon Capshaw and this bull come out of the chute and this bull's kicking up more dust than a tornado. Capshaw's gettin' bounced around silly and finally gets thrown. Now Tommy gets this bull's attention and he chases him back into the chute. Meanwhile Capshaw's on his hands and knees still tryin' to figure out which way is up. So Tommy goes on back out into the ring and gives him a hand, which is the natural thing a clown will do, only when Capshaw reaches out, on go the cuffs. Must've been two thousand people in the stands watchin' the whole thing. Boy, I only wished I'd had a camera. You should've seen the look on Capshaw's face.'

'What'd he say?' the young patrolman asked.

'Shit,' said Tommy.

'What'd you say?' the sergeant asked.

Tommy grinned. 'Nice ride.'

'Yeah, *nice ride!*' Flynn guffawed. 'And I bet it was a nice ride back to Buddy's to pick up your ten per cent of twenty-five grand for a day's work.'

'Plus gas,' Tommy added.

'So what brings you out here?' asked the patrolman.

'Well, I gotta dig a gopher out of his burrow,' Tommy said, sliding off the table and having a little trouble straightening up again.

'That back still botherin' you?' Flynn asked. 'Sure you don't want to wait till morning? You must be awful tired after that drive.'

'That's the job, though,' Tommy said, stretching. 'Track 'em and snatch 'em.' He started to move his drum box towards the booking desk.

'What's the gopher's name?' the sergeant asked.

'Randal Bates,' Tommy said.

'Never heard of him,' said the sergeant. 'What kind of indictment did he skip on?'

From his rear pocket Tommy pulled out a thin sheet of computer print-out. 'Now let's see. Looks like two counts of atrocious assault. Found his ex-wife in bed with a roadie from ZZ Top and took a tyre iron to both of them.'

'Sounds like a lovely guy,' said Flynn.

'Well,' Tommy said as he pulled a portable tape player out of the drum box, 'We'll soon see.'

Jasper was crying. Such a cute, pink baby boy, lying on the couch bawling. Lou Ann McGuinn sat at the little kitchen table in the trailer and watched him with her big blue eyes. Her soft, shiny, strawberry-blonde curls framed a face that looked almost like an angel's, sweet and pretty and full of promise. But sitting there in her trailer, watching her baby cry, Lou Ann felt like anything but an angel. That's your son, she told herself. *Your baby!* But she couldn't bring herself to move. Ever since the birth of her child it happened more and more frequently – the constant feeling that this couldn't be happening to her, that it was all a big mistake. Not Jasper, of course. He was wonderful, a treasure, the light of her life. But the rest – having no money . . . living in a broken-down trailer in a campground . . . being married to a man who was nothing more than a fool and a criminal . . . it was no good anymore. Before Jasper it had been OK. Well, not really OK, but tolerable. There had always been a remote possibility that some day, somehow her husband Roy would change, straighten out, do something right for a change. For some dumb reason – was it hope? Fear? Laziness? *Love?* – she'd stayed with him. *Stand by your man*, just like Tammy Wynette sang. Dumb, just totally dumb. He hadn't changed. Except for the worse. Especially since he'd got out of jail. As if whatever sense he'd had he'd left inside. And now she had a crying baby, and not enough baby formula or diapers, and she couldn't wait any longer.

Lou Ann picked up her crying child. She rocked him in her arms and bounced him up and down, but he didn't stop crying. Now that was a dismal feeling, wasn't it? When no amount of holding your baby, or rocking him would stop his crying. Why? Because he was hungry and wet. Because she waited too long to change him, trying to conserve the diapers as long as she could. Because she'd been diluting the formula to half the normal strength to make it last longer, just like she skimped on diapers. And it was all so her husband could use the money for drugs and beer and guns. Lou Ann rocked her baby and shook her head. I must be crazy, she thought.

She walked to the window and looked outside, just as she had done so many other times during the last three days, wondering when and if Roy would return. Parked in front of the trailer was pristine, gleaming 1957 Cadillac El Dorado convertible with its black top up. A *pink* 1957 Cadillac El Dorado convertible. Carnation Pink. Bubble-gum pink. The kind of pink that made you think of cotton candy, or Pepto-Bismol, or the inside of sea shells. Roy had bought it years ago from the widow of the man who'd lived in the trailer next door. She knew nothing about cars, and after her husband died, Roy had damn near stolen it for a few hundred dollars. This Cadillac had big shark fins with cone-shaped brake lights. It looked like it came from outer space. It was The Real Thing. But Roy's shiny pink Cadillac sat out front, unused, because he was afraid to drive it, afraid it would get scratched up. And there it was now, staring back at Lou Ann like a rebuke as she stood at the window.

How many boxes of Pampers – not those cheap store-brand diapers, but real Pampers – would that car buy? How many cases of baby formula? How many quarters for the laundry? Somehow, before the baby, she had been able to live with the idea that a stupid car was as important to Roy as she was. After all, it was a car and he was a man and Lou Ann understood that men were prone to odd relationships with their vehicles. But a stupid Cadillac was *not* more important than their baby. His as well as hers. No, that was going too far.

Jasper was still crying. Across the dirt road Lou Ann could see sweet old Mr Barton, the campground manager, go into the log cabin that served as the office. Lou Ann bit her lip and tasted lipstick. She knew what she had to do.

Wrapping Jasper in a blanket, she stepped out of the trailer and started across the dirt road. It was early evening and the sun was going down. The big spruces cast their shadows over the camp sites. Some crows cackled in the trees and a dog barked in the distance. A couple of children were playing with a red wagon on the road next to the office. Outside in the fresh air, Jasper stopped crying and Lou Ann silently rehearsed her lines.

She had just reached the office when the blast of an airhorn shattered the peaceful evening. The kids playing in the road scattered, leaving the red wagon behind. A second later Murray Waycross's pick-up came flying up the road and ran right over the wagon, flattening it with a *crunch!* Roy was in it, along with Murray and two men she didn't recognize, all hooting and shooting and carrying on like a bunch of lunatics. They were all prison buddies from Roy's latest stretch inside. She watched the truck skid to a stop next to the Cadillac, watched the men pile out and go inside the trailer. For a moment she considered going back and asking Roy for money for the baby, but that was foolish, especially when he was with his friends. Instead she turned and went into the office.

'Heaven help me,' she whispered to herself.

The office smelled of those Christmas tree-shaped scent cards Roy sometimes hung from the rear-view mirror of his Jeep, the car he'd bought so that he wouldn't have to use the Cadillac. Inside the office were two wire display racks, one filled with postcards and the other with trail and road maps. There was a big stone hearth with a deer head mounted over it, and some uncomfortable chairs made from tree branches. Behind the desk Mr Barton tipped his bifocals down on his nose and smiled.

'Evenin' Mrs McGuinn,' he said.

'Good evening to you, Mr Barton,' Lou Ann replied cheerfully.

Mr Barton was a sweet old man who looked a little like Captain Kangeroo. He had an uncanny knack for wandering into the women's showers to clean them just as she started dressing. After the first time he did it, she made a habit of tucking a towel tightly around her before she stepped out of the stall. But the truth was she really didn't care. Mr Barton was a watcher, nothing more. He lived alone and she felt a little sorry for him.

Lou Ann put Jasper on her hip, placed her free elbow on the counter and leaned forward a little. Just enough so that it would occur to Mr Barton to look, but not so much that he could see anything. Mr Barton stared for a moment, then realized what he was doing and looked up at her.

'Uh, hum, Mrs McGuinn, when are you gonna take some sun?' he asked after clearing his throat. 'This is sun country, you know . . . But you're about the palest thing in the whole damn camp.'

'One of these days, Mr Barton,' Lou Ann said wistfully. 'One of these days.'

She paused for a moment to let him stare and then said, 'Mr Barton, remember when I gave you our rent money, on the first of this month, right on time?'

'Remember it?' Mr Barton replied with a laugh. 'It's a golden day in my book of memories. First time since you and your husband came here, you actually paid the rent when it was due.'

'It was pretty surprising, wasn't it?' Lou Ann said.

'I'll say,' said Mr Barton.

Lou Ann smiled, batted her eyes, and hiked up Jasper on her hip so the manager could see him. Then, in her sweetest, most charming voice she said, 'Could I have it back?'

Mr Barton stared at her, his mouth open.

'Now, Mr Barton,' Lou Ann said. 'I wouldn't've asked you if I didn't really need it. And I could've come in here and cried and pleaded. I could've made my baby cry. But I didn't because I didn't want to ruin your day or your memories. So please, just give me the money back. My baby needs food, he needs diapers. You want to know why he's wrapped in a blanket? He doesn't have any clean clothes because I don't have any quarters for the laundry room. Please, Mr Barton? You know I wouldn't come in here begging if I wasn't desperate.'

'Well, I, uh, can't give it all back to you because I uh, don't

13

have that much here,' Mr Barton fumbled for words. 'I could, uh, let you have fifty . . . may be sixty.'

'Sixty dollars won't last me a week,' Lou Ann said. Her eyes started to get watery. 'Now I know I told you I wasn't going to cry, but if it's a choice between feeding my baby or crying I guess I'm just going to have to cry.' Lou Ann began to sniff.

'Would you take eighty?' Mr Barton asked desperately, his eyes getting watery too. 'I bet I've got that in the safe.'

Lou Ann was on the verge of saying yes. After all, Mr Barton was a nice man and she'd been brought up not to be an Indian giver. But just then Jasper began to cry. Mr Barton stared at him, and pretty soon tears were running down all three of their faces.

'Just a minute,' he said, getting up. He went into a room behind the office and Lou Ann heard him blow his nose loudly. Then he returned with a handful of bills. 'Here, please take it. Feed that poor child. Get him some clothes, for God's sake.'

Lou Ann wiped her eyes with the palm of her free hand and picked up the bills. 'Thank you, Mr Barton. You're a sweetheart.'

Mr Barton nodded and wiped the tears from his eyes.

As she walked back across the campground, Lou Ann counted the bills: $120! She could've kissed Mr Barton. But ahead of her the lights were on in the trailer, and knowing what was waiting for her inside made her quickly forget about the kindly campground manager. Roy and his friends were in there, and Roy with his friends was different than Roy alone. If Lou Ann had had any choice, she would've gone somewhere else until they left, but she was eager to get home and feed Jasper. Now that they had some money, she wasn't worried about giving him what was left of the formula . . . undiluted.

Even before she got to the trailer she could hear them inside, shouting and laughing. Lou Ann climbed the steps and went in. The trailer was filled with cigarette smoke. Roy, Murray and two other men were sitting around the kitchen table, drinking Wild Turkey. There was a plaid suitcase on the floor near the table, but Lou Ann didn't think anything of it as she went to the window and started to crank it open.

'God, Roy, you want Jasper to breath all this?' she asked.

'Sure, why the hell not?' Roy said, spreading his arms. 'Look what it's done for me.'

14

The other men laughed. Lou Ann wasn't certain what they found so funny. Holding Jasper on her hip, she went to the cupboard and took out the the can of formula. Jasper immediately began to cry. He was smart, he knew what that can meant.

To open the cupboard she'd had to transfer Mr Barton's money from her free hand to the hand she was using to hold Jasper. Without warning, Roy reached over and plucked it from her grip.

'Hey, what's this?' he asked, grinning and holding up the bills.

Lou Ann spun around, regretting that she hadn't hidden the money in her pocket. 'That's baby food money, OK? That's not for shotguns, that's not for Wild Turkey, that's not so you boys can get wasted on some kind of horse tranquilizer. Roy, you're with me on that' – she felt her voice quivering – 'right?'

Roy didn't answer. Still grinning that dumb show-off grin of his, he fanned the bills out in his hand like they were playing cards. 'This is baby-food money, boys! A hundred and twenty dollars!'

The men laughed. 'Whoa! Big deal! A hundred and twenty!'

Lou Ann watched angrily, humiliated that she'd had to beg Roy in front of them. What fools they were, each one trying to impress the next with how tough and mean he was. Had they not been there, Roy probably would've cried with joy to see that cash . . . and then taken $60 for drugs or booze. That was why she needed every penny she could get. Because half of it automatically went to him.

But then she saw something unbelievable happen. Something so stupid that it defied all rational explanation. Roy reached over and turned on the gas. He turned it up high so the flame turned blue. As Lou Ann stood there holding Jasper, trying to measure out formula for the bottle, Roy tossed the money she'd just brought home onto the burner. The bills caught fire and began to burn. Roy and his buddies laughed hysterically. Lou Ann froze. She was back in the world of the unreal. This couldn't be happening, she thought. It was a joke, a nightmare. They must've been stoned out of their minds. They were all watching her to see how she'd react. She knew they were hoping she'd get hysterical. Then Roy could slap her around a little and prove who really wore the pants in the family. Well, they were going to be disappointed.

'Uh, Roy,' she said as evenly as possible. 'Could you open the crib?'

The men grew quiet, clearly let down. Roy got up and followed her over to the fold-up crib. Behind her Murray Waycross said something she couldn't hear, and the others started to laugh again. No doubt it was something dirty. That Waycross had a filthy mind and sometimes, when Roy wasn't looking, he'd make the most digusting gestures to her. Roy leaned close to her as he opened the crib. She smelled the Wild Turkey on his breath.

'We finally got it knocked, baby,' he whispered.

Lou Ann stared at him in utter disbelief. She'd learned not to get angry. Getting angry only got him angry, and that led to fights. And yet she couldn't keep a little frustration from slipping out.

'Knocked?' She whispered back. 'Like that Amway franchise out in the desert? Like the oil-field work in Alaska? Or our famous chinchilla farm? Remember "Make fast, fast, fast cash by raising chinchillas for their pelts?" Unless you leave the cage door open and they all run away, that is.'

She was afraid he'd get mad, but instead he went back to his buddies and picked up the plaid suitcase that had been lying next to the table.

'I know I fucked up a lot of things, honey,' he said, almost singing it like a country western performer as he opened the case. 'But honest, we're on dream street now.'

There was something green inside the suitcase . . . Could it be? The men at the table were watching her with big grins on their faces. Lou Ann took a step closer. Money? The bills were in wrappers like you saw in the bank. Lou Ann stared at her husband.

'How did you make this money, Roy?'

'Oh, we didn't make it,' Roy replied, starting to grin. 'Some friends of ours did!'

The men burst out laughing again.

'Wait a minute,' Lou Ann gasped. 'Hold on. This is counterfeit money?'

Murray smiled. 'State of the fuckin art, baby.'

'This is the big time, Lou!' Roy gushed, snapping the suitcase shut. He was just like a little boy. Lou Ann grabbed him by the wrist and pulled him into the corner again.

16

'Roy, please listen to me,' she hissed under her breath. 'You did six months for selling hot VCRs. I was still here when you got out, right? I waited, Roy. But I didn't count on these prison buddies of yours. I mean, please Roy, for Jasper's sake, get rid of these psychos before they—'

'Psychos?' Roy scowled. 'These guys?'

Lou Ann glared at him. God, it was hard enough being mother to an eight-month-old baby without having to be mother to a *thirty-six-year-old* one as well.

'Hey, come on,' Roy said in the tone he used when he was trying to soften her up. 'Just let me keep the cash here a few days, just till I find a good hiding place, OK?'

Lou Ann gave him a look. Roy smiled.

'Hey,' he said. 'I know I messed up a lot of things before, but, I mean, you saw those bills. They're as real as the real thing. I swear, Lou, this one is idiot proof.'

From the time Randal Bates was a toddler, his father Everett Bates tried to leave his mark on him. In fact, Everett had left many marks on his son by beating him to within an inch of his life whenever he felt moved to by too many drinks, too little money or too much grief from whichever woman he happened to be living with at the moment. Randal's real mother had abandoned her husband and son practically at birth, but Everett was slow to catch on to things and it wasn't until Randal was eight that he realized he could abandon his son as well. For the next few years Randal was shuffled from foster home to foster home where he was abused in numerous ways before finally setting out on his own to become a model of the American life of crime.

By the time Randy introduced his ex-wife and the ZZ Top roadie to the pleasures of mutilation by tyre iron, he had been in and out of jail so many times that his police record played like a double album set. In the old days habitual criminals, were often remanded to jail without bail, but in recent years the prisons had become so overcrowded with murderers, rapists and investment bankers that the courts of law had no choice but to set high bail. Hopefully they'd be high enough to ensure the accused's return for trial, but not so high that he wouldn't be able to afford the bail bond. Thus Randy Bates had made his $10,000 bail by signing over his pickup to Buddy Donovan, the bail bondsman, who then posted the bond. Unfortunately for Buddy, when the court date rolled around, Randy had skipped and was nowhere to be found. In these situations the court usually gave the bail bondsman a simple choice: either find the fugitive or forfeit the entire bail. Hence the need for skip tracers like Tommy Nowak.

At the moment Tommy was setting his trap in the Quonset hut that served as the Rustville police station, Randy Bates was sitting in a one-room shack with a tin roof in the desert, about five miles outside of Barstow. As was his habit in the afternoons, Randy was nursing a bottle of vodka and thumbing through *The Sporting News* while trying to decide whether he would actually rob a convenience store that night, or just watch it happen on *Miami Vice*. Despite being virtually broke, he was inclined to stay in. He was fully aware that he'd missed his court date, and he knew that the fat bail bondsman Donovan, who'd stupidly accepted a hot Chevy pick-up with a phoney title as collateral, would send a skip tracer to find him. Randy doubted they'd trace him out here to the desert, but in case they did he had a Remington 12-guage pump-action loaded with buck shot by the door and a hunting knife in a sheath tied to his leg.

In the Rustville police station, Tommy was just about ready. On the table in front of him was a tape player, a telephone, a tambourine, cymbal, kazoo and whistle. Flynn, the sergeant, and the patrolman were watching him in amazement.

'How the hell you gonna get Bates with this junk?' the patrolman asked.

'Watch,' Tommy said. He picked up the receiver, dialled a number and cleared his throat.

In his shack out in the desert, Randy Bates practically jumped out of his seat at the sound of the telephone. He stared at it for several rings. Christ, who the hell knew he was out here? Must be a wrong number. Still, being cautious, Randy picked up the phone and held it to his ear without answering. He could hear all kinds of crazy noises on the other end of the line. Sounded like a party or something.

'Yellllow, is this Randy Bates?' a crazy voice asked.

Randy scowled. 'Who wants to know?'

'Yo, Randal!' the voice shouted. 'This is a crazy Karl Cummings from KZTS, the all-hits radio station, inspiration for the nation in heavy rotation at ninety-eight point nine on the digital dial. Randy, my boy, I've got a surprise for you that's just about as big as Barry Manilow's beak! Are ya sittin down, Senior Bates? Better yet, are ya lying down on a soft comfy waterbed somewhere? Huh? Are ya horizontal, Randy?'

'No,' Randy said. 'I'm sittin up. But I think I can handle it.'

In the Quonset hut Tommy laughed, hit the bell and blew on the kazoo. Flynn and the others gaped at him.

'Do you like country music, Randy, my boy?' Tommy asked in the crazy disc jockey's voice.

'Well, I used to like Roy Acuff,' Randy replied.

'Roy Acuff?' Tommy shrieked as he scratched quickly through the casettes on the table and grabbed a Dolly Parton tape. 'Well, tell the truth, Randy, will ya take Dolly Parton at a pinch? I know I would. I may be certifiable, Rand, my man, but I ain't dumb! So guess what? You're the grand prize winner, guy! You've won the KZTS phone-home prize – a night with Dolly Parton!'

Tommy pressed the play button on the tape player and Parton's 'Coat of Many Colors' started playing.

'Yes, sir,' he shouted. 'Now the phone-home prize includes a pre-show dinner for you and Miss Parton at the lovely Hawaii Kai Room of the Barstow Sheraton, a backstage pass to Dolly's big show tonight at the Barstow War Memorial, and a little dessert at Massimino's Café afterwards – but who knows if the night'll end there, Randy! She's a hot-blooded woman, partner, and she's been on the road a long, long time!'

'Well, all right!' Randy Bates shouted back.

Tommy smiled. He had his man now. 'Hey, Rand, what's your favourite radio station?'

'KZTS!' Randy shouted back.

'I can't hear you!' Tommy yelled.

'KZTS!' Randy shouted even louder.

'We'll pick you up at six in a long black limo, Batesy boy,' Tommy said. 'I'd be lookin yer best if I was you. Old Dolly likes her men fresh and clean shaven!'

'All right!' Randy shouted.

Tommy rang the bell, shook the tambourine and blew the

kazoo one more time before hanging up. He was out of breath and panting. The three officers exploded in laughter. They reeled around the Quonset hut, pounding each other on the back and cackling until they too were out of breath.

'I used to like Roy Acuff!' the sergeant gasped, mimmicking Randy. 'My lord, Tom. You turned a hardcore felon into a four-year-old boy!'

Tommy smiled, leaned back in his chair and lit a smoke.

'A night out with Dolly Parton!' Flynn yelled. 'And he fell for it!'

'Sure,' said the sergeant. 'Just think. That ole boy's been settin' out there in that shack for so long . . . He's probably so horny Tom here could've sold him on a good lookin' heifer!'

'I just can't believe the dude is sittin' out there expectin' a limousine!' the patrolman chuckled.

From outside came the toot of a finely polished car horn. Tommy grinned. 'Speak of the Devil.'

At a quarter to six they took off. Tommy, wearing the chauffeur's outfit he'd rented back in Sacramento, was driving the limo. Giving him a couple of minutes headstart were the sergeant and patrolman in the lone Rustville patrol car and Flynn in Tommy's Fury. They drove east with the red and purple desert sunset at their backs, their cars leaving plumes of dust on the dry dirt road.

The setting sun had turned Randy's wooden shack orange as Tommy pulled the limo up in front and gave the horn a toot. Randy practically burst out the front door. He was showered and cleanly shaved, wearing the cleanest jeans and western shirt he owned. Tommy hopped out and held the limo door for him.

'Evening, Mr Bates!' he said in a shrill voice. 'Congratulations!'

Randy's eyes were wide and sparkling. 'Hot damn, I ain't never won anything before!' He hopped into the back seat, rubbing his hands together. 'I am ready to par-ty hard!'

Before closing the limo door, Tommy glanced up and saw the other cars coming up the road towards them. Good timing. He ducked his head back into the limo, and took out his handcuffs.

'Randy, my name is Tom Nowak, and I have been empowered by the state of California to return you to Sacramento where you are due to stand trial for—'

Randy Bates reacted faster than Tommy had anticipated. Here was a man who clearly knew how to deal with disappointment. Before Tommy could get out of the way, Randy reared back and delivered a thrust kick to his stomach, lifting him clear out of the limo and on to the ground. Tommy landed on his back in the dust and sprang up in time to hurl himself forward, knocking Randy into the door frame of the limo. Randy pulled his hunting knife and swung wide. Tommy just managed to duck, then he smashed Randy's arm against the side of the limo. The knife went flying and, along with it, Randy's last shot at escape. Tommy hit him in the stomach with a combination and finished him with a right hook to the jaw. Randy Bates dropped to the ground face first, and Tommy pulled his arms behind him and threw the cuffs on.

'Nice,' Flynn said, getting out of the Fury. 'Very nice.'

The sergeant and patrolman got out of the patrol car and clapped as Tommy hauled Bates to his feet and threw him into the cage he'd welded into the back of the Fury. When the door was shut and locked, Tommy turned and took a bow.

'Thank you, gentlemen.'

'Haven't lost your touch,' Flynn said, patting him on the shoulder.

'The secret is staying in practice,' Tommy replied.

The patrolman leaned in the window of the Fury and sneered at Bates. 'Hey, what's your favourite radio station, Randy, my boy?'

Tommy frowned and led the younger man quickly and firmly away. 'Listen,' he said in a low voice. 'Once you catch 'em, you don't gloat. They hate that worse than goin' back to jail.'

The patrolman nodded. Tommy peeled off the chauffeur's clothes. Underneath he was still wearing his T-shirt and jeans. The sky had turned deep blue, and all that remained of the sun was a faint purplish glow in the west.

'The masked man doesn't have to ride off into the sunset, you know,' Flynn said. 'We could throw old Randy in the tank over-night and kick back for a few.'

'Would if I could, Ed,' Tommy said. 'You know that. But they want this fellow bad up north and I'd just as soon deliver him and pick up my cheque.'

'Well, then, maybe next time,' Flynn said, a little sadly.

Tommy smiled and patted him on the back. 'You take care now, chief.'

'Sure, Tommy, you too.'

Tommy got into the Fury and fired her up. On the way past the sergeant and patrolman he waved. Pretty soon he was back on the highway, heading north, the white lines of the highway glowing under the Fury's headlights. Tommy looked in the rear-view and caught Randy Bates glowering at him.

'What kind of music you want to hear, Randy?' he asked.

Bates thought about it for a moment and then smirked. 'Well, I sure don't want to hear no fuckin' Roy Acuff, I'll tell you that. I wanna here something that sounds about as mean as I feel.'

Tommy looked down at the tapes scattered on the seat beside him. He'd brought one special tape along that he thought Randy might appreciate. 'How's about some ZZ Top?'

The funky rumble of 'Cheap Sunglasses' came on and Tommy had to turn down the volume to keep Billy Gibbons and his bandmates from cracking the Fury's old speakers.

Randy Bates blinked and Tommy saw a smile creep on to his lips. The next thing he knew, Randy Bates was laughing.

2

Tommy Nowak sometimes wondered why so many states chose small and insignificant cities as their capitals. New York had Albany, Illinois had Springfield, Florida had Tallahassee. California, of course, had Sacramento.

'Easy,' Buddy Donovan answered one day. 'State politicians want to go some place where their wives won't follow.'

It occurred to Tommy that Buddy was probably right. A politician's wife with a nice house and friends in the Bay area, or down around LA or San Diego would probably not find the state capital a lot of fun. Not that there was anything particularly *wrong* with Sacramento. It had plenty of nice places to live, and the streets of its residential areas were lined with handsome elms. Besides the business of state politics, the city supported bustling banking and food-processing industries. It also had a hell of lot of lawyers, politicians and people who, like Tommy, made their livings at some offshoot of the criminal justice system.

It was just that there wasn't anything particularly *right* about Sacramento either. Located smack dab in the centre of the Sacramento Valley, it sat surrounded by flatness and growing fields. You inevitably had to get in a car and drive for an hour to find anything interesting. And in the summer the heat was merciless.

By the time Tommy got back to Sacramento and turned Randy Bates over to the authorities at the Sacramento jail, it was gaining on 2 a.m. It occurred to him that the sluggish, light-headed sensation he was experiencing might be related to a serious lack of sleep, so he drove back to the small apartment he rented on the third floor of an old Victorian house. He climbed the wooden stairs, fell face first on the bed and dove into a deep dreamless sleep.

It was close to 11 a.m before he woke up, and close to noon by the time he'd showered, shaved and changed into the first clean

23

set of clothes he'd worn in nearly a week. It was time to collect his due from Buddy Donovan, a chore that was often as challenging as tracking down the skips themselves. One thing about it was easy though. Buddy could always be found in one of two places: his office or the Courthouse Luncheonette.

Since it was lunch time, Tommy decided to first try the Luncheonette, a clean but time-worn place across from the state court-house. Through the plate-glass windows Tommy could see that it was packed with many of the smaller cogs that made the justice system run – the bailiffs and court officers, stenographers and secretaries, criminal lawyers, cops and assistant district attorneys. The fates of a lot of criminals had been decided here simply because it was a hell of a lot easier for a lawyer and a DA to plea bargain a defendant over coffee and Danish than in front of some over-worked judge.

As Tommy entered the establishment heads turned, most of them extending greetings. Like a politician, Tommy acknowledged them but kept moving. His goal was Buddy, sitting at his regular table in the back, a broad white napkin spread out neatly over his shirt, tie and checked sports jacket. Buddy already knew Tommy was coming. He had the most well-developed sixth sense Tommy had ever seen. It was a sense that told him whether money was going to be made or lost. Buddy could always tell when Tommy was around because it meant both.

'Say hey!,' Buddy said by way of a greeting, looking up as Tommy approached. 'It's my favourite bloodhound.'

Tommy stopped at the table and nodded at Buddy's companions, two new skip tracers named Cal and Zack. Then he turned to Buddy.

'Listen,' Tommy said. 'I just did Randy Bates and I'd like the cash, if you have it.'

'You did Bates?' Cal gasped. 'How?'

Normally Tommy would've answered, but he knew that was just what Buddy wanted, a distraction from the real business at hand.

'Have you got it on you, Buddy?' Tommy asked.

The waitress arrived at the table, tapping her pencil on her order pad. Buddy patted the seat next to him. 'Hey, we're just ordering. Sit down.'

Tommy hestitated. The way Buddy ate, that could mean the whole afternoon. 'Thanks, but I got things to do.'

'You gotta eat for Christ's sake,' Buddy said. When Tommy still wouldn't sit, he turned to the waitress. 'Lemme have a Chief Justice Warren Burger, well done, extra fries.'

The waitress nodded and turned to the short-order cook behind the grill. In a nasal voice she shrieked, 'One Warren, burn it!'

Buddy slapped his menu closed and tucked the napkin a little more tightly into the collar of his shirt.

'Pay me now, Buddy,' Tommy said, feeling impatient. 'I got to go visit somebody.'

'Visit?' Buddy chortled and his jowls jiggled. 'You gotta visit someone? Funny, I never saw Tom Nowak as the type to go out paying polite little social calls.'

Buddy thought this was so funny he started to laugh. Cal and Zack smiled kind of nervously. They might have depended on Buddy for some of their work, but they weren't about to laugh at Tommy. Tommy just stood there staring at Buddy. It was funny how a good hard look always cut Buddy's laughter short.

'OK, OK,' Buddy mumbled and dug into his pocket. He pulled out a wad of bills and placed it on the table. Tommy picked them up and started counting.

'This ain't all of it, Buddy,' Tommy said when he'd finished.

'It ain't?' Buddy pretended to be surprised. 'Well, let's see now. Ten per cent of ten thousand is, uh, how do you like that?'

'I don't, Buddy,' Tommy said. 'Now how about it?'

'Well, how's about you comin' by the office for the rest later this afternoon, OK?' Buddy said. 'I ain't exactly a walkin' ATM machine.'

'I'll be there,' Tommy said.

As he turned to leave, Zack called out behind him. 'Come on, Tom, how'd you do Randy Bates?'

Tommy waved and smiled. He wasn't about to give away any professional secrets. He had just reached the door when another voice called out, 'He tricked the poor bastard, that's what he did. Suckered him, snuck up on him when he was half-delirious over some fantasy about Dolly Parton.'

Tommy spun around in the doorway. The speaker was a young

25

guy in a dark suit. A frisky boy lawyer. Tommy could smell them a mile away. 'What's it to you?' he asked.

'I'm his lawyer,' the young attorney said. 'And I'll tell you this, Nowak. There's a pretty thin line between what you do and what some outlaws do.'

The whole diner fell silent. It was a rare moment when anyone confronted Tommy Nowak so brazenly. Tommy sized the guy up and knew he could take him with both hands tied behind his back and his right leg in a cast. That wasn't the point here, though. So instead he let a little smile slide across his lips.

'Yeah,' he said in a quiet voice the patrons had to strain to hear. 'It's a thin line . . . but it ain't invisible.'

It took a moment, but then the whole place broke up. By then Tommy was out the door.

They'd left just after midnight. Roy, Murray and the other two. Lou Ann was glad to see them go. She was even glad to see Roy go. She would've been sad had he been the old Roy, that somewhat lovable, ne'er do well husband of hers. But this new Roy was someone else. Six months inside had done something to him, changed him somehow. The last traces of decency and common sense had been washed away with industrial-strength stupidity. These men he was fooling with now truly frightened her. They had a look, a smell that said they were not only ruthless, but maybe even a bit insane as well.

Murray was away talking about something called the Birthright. The name rang some kind of little gong in Lou Ann's head, but she couldn't quite place it. She tried to convince herself that it was nothing. Murray just had a big mouth – he was only trying to make himself look important. Intuition, however, told her it was danger. All these drugs and guns and insanity . . . Lou Ann knew it had rubbed off on Roy, and she was petrified that it might rub off on Jasper as well.

Using Scotch tape and scissor, Lou Ann had managed to salvage about $50 from the scorched bills Roy had tossed on the stove the night before. If anyone looked closely they might discover that the serial numbers on the left sides of the bills didn't always match those on the right, but she doubted anyone would notice. The next morning she bundled up Jasper and caught a ride into town with a neighbour to buy diapers and baby food.

Later, riding back into the campground she'd noticed the black sedan parked outside the camp office and the two men in raincoats standing at the door talking to Mr Barton. And hadn't he given her the funniest look as she rode by? But Lou Ann didn't think much of it. Her thoughts were on getting home, feeding Jasper and doing the laundry. There was another sedan parked under the trees across from the trailer with two more men in it. Again Lou Ann noticed, but it didn't alarm her. She carried Jasper and the boxes of diapers and bags of groceries up the steps and inside. The trailer still smelled of urine and smoke, and the dirty glasses and empty bottles were still on the table. Lou Ann made Jasper a bottle and put him in the crib, then set about cleaning the place up. During the six months Roy was inside she'd gotten used to living by herself. If it wasn't for the problem of money, she was beginning to think she just might enjoy it.

The sink was filled with soapy water and she was in the middle of doing the dishes when she heard the knock.

'Who is it?'

'US Secret Service, Mrs McGuinn. We'd appreciate it if you'd open the door.'

Lou Ann felt a wave of fright. Like a chill it washed over her, leaving goose bumps. The Secret Service! What on earth could they want with her? Without even taking off her rubber gloves, she turned to the door and pulled it open. She stared, open-mouthed as a man in a raincoat held a folded sheet of paper towards her. Behind him were more men in raincoats. One of them was holding a shotgun.

The man in the raincoat tried to hand her the papers, but Lou Ann was still too shocked to move.

'This is a federal search warrant, Mrs McGuinn,' the man said. 'We have reason to believe that there is counterfeit money in this trailer.'

Lou Ann's heart was beating so hard she thought it might crack her ribcage. 'There . . . there is, right there,' she stammered, pointing at the plaid suitcase. 'But it's not mine.'

The Secret Service man looked at the suitcase. 'Would you mind if we came in, Mrs McGuinn?'

'No, of course not. I mean the place is awful messy, but . . .'

It was obvious that the Secret Service was not there to inspect the cleanliness of her trailer. They huddled around the suitcase and pulled it open. Meanwhile, the man with the shotgun stood in the doorway, watching for anyone coming from outside.

The Secret Service men peered into the suitcase, picking up the stacks of bills and mumbling to each other. Finally one of the men turned to her.

'If this money isn't yours, Mrs McGuinn, could you tell us who it belongs to?'

Lou Ann opened her mouth to speak, but caught herself. Roy. His so-called friends. The Birthright. She knew what those men were . . . they were angry, vengeful, crazed killers. Her life wouldn't be worth a plug nickel if she turned them in. They'd kill her. They'd kill Jasper. She suddenly felt light headed, and had to lean against the counter to steady herself.

'Uh, Mrs McGuinn?' the Secret Service man said.

'I can't tell you,' Lou Ann replied. 'I mean, I'd like to, but I can't.'

The Secret Service man looked at the others and frowned.

'Uh, Mrs McGuinn,' he said, 'let me explain something to you. We know that this campsite is registered in your name, as is this trailer. That means that unless you tell us otherwise, we have to assume that this money belongs to you and that you are therefore in violation of some very serious laws against counterfeiting. Do you understand?'

'Do counterfeiters get the chair?' Lou Ann asked.

'Well no, but . . .' the startled Secret Service man began to answer.

'Then I'm guilty,' Lou Ann said quickly regaining her composure. She pointed at the crib where Jasper was still sucking happily on his bottle. 'Now what about my baby?'

'Well, uh, I guess we'll contact the state social services department,' the Secret Service man said.

A warning siren went off in Lou Ann's mind. She knew what happened to those social services kids. They got put into foster homes. They were abused and maltreated, and often wound up on the streets.

'The hell you will,' Lou Ann said. She stripped off her rubber gloves and went to the phone and dialled the number of her sister Dinah over in Carson City.

The Secret Service man reached toward her. 'I'm sorry, Mrs McGuinn, but you can't use the phone at a time like this.'

Lou Ann jumped back, pulling the phone away from him. 'The hell I can't,' she snapped. 'Now you just listen to me. I may be going to jail, but my son is not going into any social services. I'll be with you in just a moment, but first I'm going to take care of him.'

On the other end, the phone was ringing. Finally Dinah answered.

'Dinah, it's Lou Ann. Listen, hon, I'm in a terrible jam and I need your help. Could you drive on over here and take Jasper for a while?'

'Sure, but what's wrong?' Dinah asked.

'It's a long story,' Lou Ann said. 'I can't explain now because some men are waiting for me. You know the office on the left just as you come into campground?'

'Yes?'

'Well, go in there and ask for Mr Barton. He's a sweet old man, and I'm going to leave Jasper with him till you get here. I'll leave you all the bottles and diapers too.'

'OK,' Dinah said. 'But how long do you think you'll be?'

Lou Ann put her hand over the phone and turned to the Secret Service men. 'What do counterfeiters usually get?' she asked.

A couple of them scratched their heads. 'I don't know. Five to eight, fifteen to twenty-five. Depends on your record.'

'Well, I don't have a record and I intend to be a model prisoner,' Lou Ann said.

'Well, you could get off after three years with good behaviour I suppose,' said one of the Secret Service men.

'Great,' Lou Ann said, getting back on the phone. 'Listen, Dinah, I should be back for him before kindergarten.'

'Huh?'

'Don't take me too serious, hon, I'm just a little excited.' Lou Ann hung up and turned back to the Secret Service men. 'Now if one of you gentlemen would take that box of Pampers over to the campground office, I'll fix up a batch of bottles and take the baby and we can get this show on the road.'

At three in the afternoon Tommy stopped in front of DONOVAN'S BAIL BONDS. Painted on the plate glass window below the name was:

DON'T CALL YOUR WIFE OR HUSBAND
THEY MIGHT NOT WANT YOU OUT
WE GET YOU OUT IN MINUTES
MASTERCARD AND VISA WELCOMED

Tommy pushed the door open and went in. The place looked more like a pawn shop than a bail bondsman's office. TVs, stereos, ornate cowboy saddles and other paraphernalia taken as collateral against bonds was piled in heaps. Tommy made his way towards the back where Buddy was on the phone.

'Look, Mrs Litowinsky,' Buddy was shouting into the receiver. 'I don't care how late your son was up last night, if he ain't in court in one hour they're gonna issue a warrant for his arrest . . . What? Hey, Mrs Litowinsky, that ain't nothin' compared to what I'm gonna do if he puts that bail bond in jeopardy, you understand?' Buddy glanced up at Tommy and winked. 'That's right, Mrs Litowinsky, I got a bounty hunter here who don't even speak English. All he does is grunt and beat the livin' shit out of anybody he brings in . . . What? How many times your son's nose been broken, Mrs Litowinsky? Never? Well, this skip tracer ain't never brought a man in without havin' his nose broken . . . Assault? Hell no. He never touches them. This may sound strange, but they always break their noses on the doorframe of the car. Ain't that peculiar, Mrs Litowinsky? . . . Yeah, I think so too. I know your son needs his rest, but I bet he needs his nose even more . . . That's right, Mrs Litowinsky, you go roust him up and tell him to be in court in one hour. Thanks, Mrs Litowinsky. Yeah, you have a nice day too.'

Buddy hung up the phone and shook his head. 'You imagine that? His momma doesn't want him to go to court unless he's had a good night's sleep! You see the world workin' that way? "Sorry, boss, can't come to work today because I didn't have a good night's sleep." Jesus, what's wrong with these people?'

'As I recall I'm here 'cause you owe me, Buddy,' Tommy said, moving some papers out of the way and sitting down on the corner of an old wooden desk.

'Sure do have a way of cuttin' through the bullshit, don't you, Tom?' Buddy smirked and pulled open a drawer. He took out the balance of Tommy's pay and handed it to him.

Tommy thumbed through the money and folded it into his pocket. He hopped off the table, full of raw energy. 'So what've you got for me, Buddy?'

'What've I got?' Buddy scowled. 'Christ almighty Tom, first you come in here breakin' my nuts about gettin' paid, then you turn right around and ask for work!?'

Tommy grinned. 'So what else is new?'

'OK, OK. Skips? Well, I got little Walter Drucker, the schmuck who gave me that defective microwave for collateral. He's sitting downtown in the Golden Bear Motel just waitin' to be plucked like some fuckin' apple on a tree.'

'Give him to one of the kids,' Tommy said, waving the idea away. 'There's no fun in the Walter Druckers of the world.'

'No fun,' Buddy repeated, exasperated. 'Jesus F. Christ. Most guys think this is a job, but Mr Bring-'Em-Back-Alive needs a big fun fix.'

Tommy realized he was pacing around the office. He'd had a good night's sleep, a good meal, and he was raring to go. Randy Bates was past history. He needed something to do today.

'If I may quote the immortal Olivia Newton John,' Buddy said, watching him. 'Have you never been mellow?'

Tommy smirked at him.

'Have you never *tri-ee-eye-eyed* . . .?' Buddy sang.

Tommy lifted a tagged .38 police special from the shelf, aimed it at Buddy and pulled the trigger. He heard the scratch of flint and a small flame burst from the barrel. Tommy stared at it for a moment, then pulled out a cigarette and lit it.

'I know what you can do,' Buddy said, pulling open a drawer and lifting out a handful of yellow forms. 'Why don't you fill out these mileage reports and justify all the money I spend on gasoline for you?'

Tommy toyed with the lighter.

'Why don't you do that?' Buddy asked. 'Hey! I asked you a question.'

Tommy gazed back at him. 'And I didn't answer.'

'So, you could do Walter Drucker,' Buddy said, throwing his hands up in disgust. 'But fuck that, it's no fun. You could fill out mileage reports, but fuck that, it's too much like a real job. You could fuck that gorgeous stenographer, Mary Ellen Chesbro, who's been mooning after you for two years, but *fuck that* . . . she might get her hooks into you. Look. Do Drucker. For once in your life, Tom, would you try to do something reasonable?'

Tommy put the gun down and smiled. 'I tried it once. I didn't care for it.'

He headed for the door.

'Where're you going?' Buddy asked.

'Don't know,' Tommy said. 'But if anything good comes up, I bet you'll find me.'

3

Lou Ann had been in a courtroom once before in her life, and that was the day Roy's possession of stolen-property-with-intent-to-sell case got plea bargained down to a class D felony, six to nine months in jail and five years' probation. It did not escape her now that were he to be charged with counterfeiting while still on probation, the judge would be compelled to throw the maximum sentence at him. And while half of Lou Ann believed the maximum sentence was just what her fool husband deserved, the other half said he was still her husband. He was possibly even still a good human being if you dug deep enough and drained off all the drugs and booze, and he was definitely still the father of Jasper, who, like any boy growing up, would need a father figure around.

Having spent the previous night in the holding tank, Lou Ann was frisked, finger-printed, photographed and otherwise processed through the entry levels of the criminal justice system. She now stood in a courtroom at the counsel table, sandwiched between Whitney, a young, court-appointed lawyer, in a blue business suit, and a young man in a similar suit named Hastings, who was the district attorney assigned to the case. In front of her sat the judge, who had a moustache and longish hair, and who looked much younger than she had expected him to look. In the seats behind her were Roy, Murray Waycross and several of their buddies. The court officers, the DA and the judge kept glancing back warily at them.

The DA read the charges against her while the judge listened and rubbed his chin, just like the judges on TV did.

'Now doesn't it seem just a little strange,' the judge said, 'that Mrs McQuinn, who has no previous criminal record at all, is the only one being indicted for possession of this counterfeit money?'

DA Hastings cleared his throat. 'Your Honour, she was the

only person home at the time of the raid, and she steadfastly refuses to tell us anything about the crime.'

'One can hardly blame the woman, Mr Hastings,' the judge replied. 'After all, she's got a Folsom Prison class reunion going on right behind her.'

Roy's friends snickered and chuckled. Lou Ann reached nervously into her pocket and rubbed her thumb against the fob of Roy's extra set of keys. On the way out of the trailer with the Secret Service men the day before, she'd been so nervous and upset that she couldn't find her own set, and had taken his. Meanwhile, Ms Whitney spoke to the judge: 'If Your Honour pleases, the gentlemen have come to post bond for the defendant.'

'I believe it's called hush money, counsellor,' the judge replied with a chuckle.

'Your Honour,' DA Hastings said. 'We have reason to believe that the counterfeit money found in Mrs McGuinn's possession is only the proverbial tip of the iceberg. Other crimes and monies are definitely involved here, and we would ask the court to set bond with that fact in mind.'

'But you're not saying that Mrs McGuinn is involved in those crimes,' the judge replied.

'We have no evidence of that, Your Honour,' the DA said, 'but it may be necessary for her to appear in the future as a material witness.'

The judge pondered the situation and then said, 'The court sets bail at twenty-five thousand dollars.'

There was some shuffling in the seats, and Lou Ann turned to see Murray Waycross rise with a big dumb-ass grin on his face.

'We'll cover that action, baby,' he shouted. Roy and the others cheered and hooted. Thinking quickly, Lou Ann realized that if she allowed those men to pay her bail she would be indebted to them. The implications could be quite unsavoury. She whispered something to Ms Whitney, who listened and nodded.

'Your Honour,' Ms Whitney said. 'Mrs McGuinn would prefer to seek bail from a recognized bail bondsman.'

The judge's eyebrows went up. 'Oh? Why is that, Mrs McGuinn?'

'Well, Your Honour,' Lou Ann said hesitantly. 'I just want to be real, real careful about who I owe my freedom to.'

'I can understand that,' the judge said, banging his gavel down. 'The court clerk will make the appropriate arrangements with a certified bail bondsman. Good luck, Mrs McGuinn.'

'Thanks, Your Honour.'

The certified bail bondsman in this case was a tubby, lecherous fellow named Donovan who spent more time trying to look down Lou Ann's blouse than he did inspecting the diamond engagement ring she gave him as collateral. Lou Ann was a bit surprised at how little remorse she felt in giving up the ring. It had been given to her by Roy's grandmother, who'd told her it had been in the family for more generations than anyone could remember. Lou Ann had expected tears, but what she felt was more akin to relief, as if she were severing some old leftover ties.

'This is supposed to be collateral for a twenty-five-thousand-dollar bail bond?' Buddy asked sceptically.

'Please, Mr Donovan, it's all I've got,' Lou Ann implored him. She watched one of his eyebrows go up and knew immediately what he was thinking. God, they all thought alike, didn't they?

'You don't think there's *anything else* you could, uh, give to secure this bond?' Buddy asked, his eyes again glued to her body.

'Mr Donovan, I am an honest, moral person,' Lou Ann said. 'You and I both know I'm innocent. I'm only covering up for my husband and his friends because if I don't, quite frankly, I might as well throw myself in the Sacramento River right now. My husband's running with those people, the Birthright, you've heard of them?'

Buddy's eyes widened for a moment and he nodded.

'So you understand what I'm up against,' Lou Ann said. 'And you know that if you do not help me I will have to sit in jail until my trial. I have an eight-month-old son, Mr Donovan, and even as I sit here with you it's breaking my heart that I'm not with him. Do you want me to sit in jail, Mr Donavan? Is that really what you want?'

Buddy sighed. Ninty-nine point nine per cent of his clients claimed they were innocent, but for some strange reason he believed her. God knows he'd heard enough sob stories in his life to turn his heart to stone, but this one got to him. Just a sucker for a pretty woman, he guessed.

'You wouldn't happen to have a photograph of yourself, would you?' Buddy asked.

Lou Ann scowled, but she wasn't in a position to argue. She dug through her bag and came up with a Polaroid of herself wearing a sweatshirt and cut-off jeans, cooking dinner and holding Jasper. Her hair was pulled back in a ponytail. Not the greatest picture, but she had a feeling it didn't matter. She slid it across the desk to him.

Buddy picked it up and studied it for a moment, then slipped it into the top drawer of his desk.

'OK,' he said, 'this is what I'm gonna do for you, Mrs McGuinn. I'm gonna post your bond. But, I want you to know two things. First, this ring ain't worth a thousand dollars and I'm a goddamned fool for taking it on a twenty-five thousand bond. However, I believe you got a bad rap, and as hard-assed as I am, I don't want to see you separated from your child. Now if I do this, I want a promise from you. You said before that you and your husband live in a trailer out in some campground?'

Lou Ann nodded.

'All right,' Buddy said. 'I want you back here at 9 a.m. tomorrow morning with the title to the trailer. You understand? Not 9.15. Not 9.30. Nine a.m. Clear?'

Lou Ann nodded again.

'OK,' Buddy said. 'Now the second thing is this. So help me God if you don't show up here at 9 a.m. tomorrow morning I am gonna assume you've skipped, and that being the case I am gonna send out the best goddamn skip tracer I have to find you and bring you back. Birthright or no Birthright. Even if he has to bring you back piece by piece. Understand?'

Lou Ann nodded for the third time.

'Well, then,' Buddy said, getting up. 'That's it. I'll see you here at 9 a.m. And when you see your son, give him a big kiss for me.'

A few hours later Roy and Lou Ann walked up the dirt road past the campground office and toward their trailer. Roy's friends had taken off somewhere, leaving them to take public transportation back from the court. The pink Cadillac was still parked out front, along with Roy's old Jeep. As they neared the trailer, Roy put his arm around Lou Ann's shoulder. She felt a chill. My, she thought, how our feelings change.

'Why didn't you let 'em go your bail, babe?' Roy asked. 'You know they're good for it.'

'I'm sorry,' Lou Ann said. 'I just couldn't let your, uh, friends, do it.'

'But they don't mind,' Roy said. 'They understand. They're, like, deep.'

Lou Ann glanced at him sceptically.

'I mean it,' Roy said. 'You'll love 'em once we get up to the camp.'

'I just want to see my baby,' Lou Ann said. They reached the trailer and stopped. Lou Ann stood next to the pink Cadillac and ran her fingers over the hood. Roy's pride and joy. In all the years he'd had it, she'd never been able to figure out whether it was the ugliest, or most beautiful, thing she'd ever seen.

'Tell you what,' Roy said. 'We'll pick him up at your sister's house and then head on up to the camp all together, OK?'

'Sure, Roy,' Lou Ann said, smiling weakly. 'Maybe you'll even have the Cadillac tuned up in time for the ride.'

'Forget about it, Lou,' Roy said, reaching over and removing her hand from the car's hood. 'This is a museum piece. It's too precious to drive.'

Lou Ann looked at him in disbelief. There's something very wrong with this man's priorities, she thought. Across the road she noticed Mr Barton coming toward her, waving. Meanwhile, Roy started into the trailer.

'Well?' he said. 'I'm starved. You makin' lunch?'

'You go ahead,' Lou Ann said. 'I'll just say hello to Mr Barton for a minute.'

Roy disappeared into the trailer and Lou Ann glanced again at the Cadillac. The seed of an idea was beginning to grow in her mind, but it was so portentous that she didn't think she'd ever have the guts to go through with it. She ran her fingers along the hood of the car again, then withdrew her hand quickly as Mr Barton joined her.

'Your sister came for the baby,' he said. 'Everything went OK, I think. I just stuck a bottle in his mouth everytime he started to yelp.'

'Thanks, Mr Barton, you really helped me out,' Lou Ann said. The idea was still in her head. She reached into her pocket. It was just dumb luck that she had Roy's keys.

'I sure was sorry to hear about the arrest,' Mr Barton said. 'You think they're gonna take the baby away? I mean, after they find you guilty and all?'

'I don't know, Mr Barton,' Lou Ann said. The idea had now swollen to giant proportions. Why should she go to jail for that fool? Why should she let the social services have her child? Why not just run? Get in the car, get Jasper and *GO*! She glanced quickly back at the trailer, then pulled open the Cadillac's door and slid into the driver's seat. The black and white leather gave comfortably, but her feet didn't quite reach the pedals. Mr Barton leaned in the window.

'Sure is a fine machine,' he said, wistfully. 'Every boy's dream, huh? A pink Cadillac.'

Lou Ann placed her hands on the steering wheel. 'You know what Elvis said. "You may go to college, You may go to school, You may drive a pink Cadillac, But don't you be nobody's fool."'

They both laughed. Lou Ann reached down and adjusted the driver's seat forward.

'Roy never drove this thing,' she said. 'Never even had the top down.' She glanced up at Mr Barton. 'And you ask me why I never get any sun on my face?'

She took the keys out of her pocket and stuck the appropriate one into the ignition. In the window Mr Barton cleared his throat.

'Uh, not that I want to interfere in your marriage, Mrs McGuinn, but it's dangerous to mess with a man's vehicles.'

'You're right about that, Mr Barton,' Lou Ann said. She turned the key in the ignition, but nothing happened. She tried again and the motor turned over once and coughed. On the third try, it suddenly caught. Lou Ann blinked. She could hardly believe it herself. She revved the engine and the big car rocked ever so slightly. Mr Barton backed away, glancing nervously at the trailer. Well, you're in it now, Lou Ann told herself, as she pulled the gear lever on the steering column into drive.

The Cadillac heaved itself forward, and Lou Ann cranked the wheel around to straighten it on the dirt road. She waved back at

Mr Barton and felt a thrill like nothing she could remember since the senior prom when Danny O'Shea asked her for the first dance. As she passed the campground office she looked in the rear-view mirror and saw Roy burst out of the trailer, waving his arms and screaming bloody murder. Lou Ann pressed her foot to the floor and felt the Caddy accelerate. There was no doubt in her mind that he'd be coming after her.

Roy McGuinn's earliest memories were of things slipping through his fingers. At the age of five his mother's favorite plate had slipped through his fingers, and she'd hauled him off and whacked him good across the side of the head. At the age of twelve an ant farm at school had slipped through his fingers, releasing three hundred red fire ants in the classroom and resulting, in the following weeks, in numerous inflamed bites to the children in his class. For this he was beaten up on a regular basis after school by those bitten. At the age of eighteen the football had slipped through his fingers on a catch which, had he made it, would have sent his highschool team to the state championships. Many things had slipped through his fingers since then: jobs, pills, bottles of booze, opportunities.

But this . . . this was the worst. In one fell swoop he had let both the biggest deal and the dearest, most important possession in his life slip through his fingers. The only thing he had left, the only thing he felt close to. And to think his wife was driving it. There was no doubt in his mind that she knew what was in the pink Cadillac. Somehow she'd found out. He didn't know how, but he was certain she knew.

'SHIT!' Roy screamed at the top of his lungs as he jumped into the Jeep and took off after her. He had to get that car back. Christ, his goddamn life depended on it. By now the Cadillac was just a plume of dust way down the road. Roy ground the Jeep through its gears, got it up to full speed and reached under the seat to make sure his .45 was there. Damn right it was.

Way up ahead he saw the Cadillac slow down and turn off the dirt road and get on the highway. Roy kept the Jeep floored, banging down through the ruts and potholes like a banshee. He thought he could catch her on the highway. Lou Ann was such a cautious driver. Her idea of high speed was fifty-six miles an hour.

A few moments later Roy made the turn on to the highway. He could just make out the Cadillac up ahead, passing the fast-food places and car dealers on either side. Now that he was on pavement he just about pushed the pedal through the floor, the wind whipping his hair around like crazy, making the sleeves of his shirt flap. Sure enough he was gaining on her. He could't imagine what damn fool notion had gotten into Lou Ann's head, thinking she could get away like this. But it really didn't matter anyway. She'd dicked with him and the Birthright, and that was that. Wasn't it?

He was really gaining on her now. In less than a mile he figured he'd be alongside the Caddy. Fuckin' Alex would like that. Yeah, he could make himself into a hero with the Birthright. The man who cut down his own wife for what she had done. Of course, it was murder, but Alex said they were outlaws, right? Well, Roy thought, maybe he'd play it safe and just shoot out the tires.

Up ahead on the right was a mall with some kind of gathering going on. As Roy got closer he could see some jackass evangelist in the parking lot standing up on an RV with a big painting of Jesus on the side and the slogan 'JESUS GOES EVERYWHERE'. A crowd had gathered around the RV and the evangelist was exhorting them through one goddamn loud sound system. His words came with the wind into the open Jeep: 'For the Son of God dwells in the humblest of places! Why, you might even see Jesus in the Stop 'N' Shop, comin' down aisle six! You might see Jesus standing at the pump down at the Sunoco station! Why Jesus . . .'

By now the Jeep was right on the Caddy's tail. Roy reached under the seat for the .45. Well, he hated the idea of shooting the tyres. Maybe he'd shoot *over* her. Just scare her good. Teach her who was boss and not to dick with the Birthright. Suddenly Lou Ann hung a sharp right into the parking lot and Roy followed, the jeep going up on two wheels around the corner. The crowd scattered. People were screaming, pointing, running in every direction. It looked to Roy like Lou Ann was gonna run his pride and joy right into the side of that goddamn RV!

At the last possible second Lou Ann turned away. Roy couldn't react soon enough. The RV loomed large in his face. He hit the brakes, the tyres screeched, son-of a bitch!

There was a tremendous crash. Then silence and the sound of tinkling glass and groaning metal. Roy blinked. His head was throbbing. The Jeep was half submerged under the rear of the RV. The windshield looked like a spider's web covered with dew. He felt something warm drip down his forehead and heard the screech of the Cadillac's tyres spinning on some sand as Lou Ann pulled back on to the highway. Son of a bitch. Roy wiped the blood off his face. *Son of a bitch!*

He grabbed the .45 and jumped out of the Jeep. The goddamn RV was the only thing with wheels in sight, and if he didn't catch that Cadillac it was gonna cost him his life, or worse. The evangelist was coming towards him.

'Son,' the evangelist started to say, 'I want to tell you what Jesus would do in a situation like this. Why he'd . . .'

'Gimme the keys,' Roy shouted, aiming the .45 at his evangelical face. '*Gimme the goddamn keys!*'

The evangelist quickly reached into his pocket and tossed Roy the keys. Roy jumped into the RV, threw it into gear, and took off.

Too late, she was gone. Sitting up high in the seat of the RV, Roy could see clear down the highway, and there was no sign of the Cadillac. Roy slowed down and pulled the RV off the road. No sense in getting pinched for stealing the damn thing. He had bigger things to worry about now. He jumped out of the RV and ran to a phone booth outside a liquor store and dialled Murray's number. While he waited for Murray to answer the phone, he leaned forward and pressed his forehead against the window of the phone booth.

'Oh, Roy,' he muttered. 'Oh, Roy, what are you gonna do now?'

'Yeah-llow?' Murray answered.

'Murray,' Roy gasped. 'Murray, she took it!'

'The Caddy?'

'Yeah,' Roy said.

'Holy shit, boy, your ass is grass. When Alex finds out he's gonna have you ground into hamburger. Oh, boy, just wait till . . .'

'Would you shut up?' Roy begged. 'Do me a favour. Get in your pick-up and get the hell out here. I'm on Route 49, at the liquor store about a mile past the last mall. Maybe we can still find her.'

'Well, I'd like to help you out, Roy,' Murray said. 'But I can't.'

'Why the hell not?' Roy asked.

'Well, *American Bass Fisherman* just came on and you know how I hate to miss that show.'

Roy couldn't believe his ears. 'Jesus Christ, Murray. You know what Alex is gonna do to me if I don't find that Cadillac. How the hell can you sit there and watch some goddamn fishing show when my life is on the line?'

'Listen, calm down,' Murray said. 'It's only a half hour. I'll be out there soon enough and we'll give her a look, OK?'

'Well, I guess,' Roy said.

'Atta boy, Roy.' Murray hung up.

So Roy sat by the side of the road and waited. When he saw the police cruiser coming down the highway he scrambled down into a ditch and hid behind some rabbit brush. The cruiser pulled over next to the RV, and the evangelist and some cops got out and looked everything over. They stood there talking and nodding their heads, and Roy squatted behind the brush and watched a scorpion trying to struggle out of a spider's web while the spider waited nearby.

Finally the evangelist got into the RV and he and the cops drove off. In the web, the scorpion stopped struggling and the spider started sucking its juices. Roy thought about sucking some juices himself and went up to the liquor store to buy a pint of Wild Turkey.

He had just about finished the bourbon when Murray's pick-up truck came cruising by. Roy flagged him down and got in.

'How was *American Bass Fisherman*?' Roy sulked.

'Great!' Murray said. 'Boy, they sure do catch some lunkers on that show. By the way, seen any sign of her?'

Roy shook his head slowly. The sun was starting to go down and with it his hopes of finding Lou Ann or the Cadillac.

'Well,' Murray said, pulling the pick-up back on to the highway. 'You just explain everything to Alex, and Alex will pass judgement on it.'

'Yeah, sure.' Roy chewed on his thumb nail. His brain was foggy with bourbon and lack of sleep. 'Listen, Murray, I am worn out and shitfaced. You got any speed around here?'

Murray reached into his shirt pocket and pulled out a small yellow cardboard box. Roy stared at it.

'Dexatrim?' he scowled. 'What the hell am I supposed to do with a supermarket diet pill?'

'Gobble up the box far as I'm concerned,' Murray said, ''cause I ain't gonna waste good crystal on you now. Maybe after we find Lou Ann.'

Roy shrugged, tore open the box and chowed down.

Lou Ann needed a place to hide. There was no way she could outrun Roy. She just couldn't stand driving that fast. Even when he'd crashed the Jeep into that Winnebego she wasn't relieved. She knew if he could he'd steal some other car and come after her. God, if only he'd felt for her what he felt for this stupid Cadillac.

The hiding place she'd finally found was an abandoned drive-in a little ways off the highway. The entrance was almost hidden behind weeds and brush. Whoever had last owned it hadn't even bothered to take the red plastic letters off the marquee when they'd left, although time and the elements had knocked off a few. What remained said:

SATU DA N GHT FE ER
OHN TR V TA

So she knew how long ago the last show had been. Lou Ann drove the Cadillac slowly over the cracked macadam with weeds and wildflowers growing through the crevices, past the long rows of rusty speaker poles. Even the big drive-in screen had started to deteriorate. Some of the plywood panels were coming loose, and she caught glimpses of the wooden supports behind it. She drove behind the screen and parked. Even if Roy decided to look in the drive-in for her, he'd have to come all the way across the lot and behind the screen. And somehow, knowing him, she wasn't too worried.

She sat back and stared again at the marquee. *Saturday Night Fever*. God, she'd still been at San Bernardino Community College when that movie had swept the country. She'd been studying to be an executive secretary. Oh, the fantasies she'd had, sitting in those stuffy classrooms, learning things like word processing and the correct way to answer a telephone. She'd pictured herself someday in a big glass-lined office building in San Francisco with her own desk, the model of neatness and efficiency, wearing glasses and a smart-looking suit. And every once in a while her boss would come out with some very important business associate and they'd pass her desk and her boss would say, 'See this little lady here? Without her I'd be lost.'

Lou Ann shook her head and smiled at the memory. Oh, it could have been. It really could have. If only she hadn't fallen in love with a handsome boy named Roy McGuinn. A handsome boy who'd turned out to be such a fool. Lou Ann yawned. She was tired. The thrill of escaping had exhausted her. She lay down on the wide leather seat and rested her head in her arms. In her wildest fantasies she'd even imagined her boss one day promoting her to senior vice-president. Lou Ann smiled and closed her eyes, wondering whatever happened to drive-in movies anyway?

4

At ten a.m. the next morning, Buddy sat at his desk and stared at a grandfather clock he'd taken as collateral from a young man who'd beaten up his invalid grandmother for drug money. 'I am a horse's ass,' he mumbled to himself. 'A true horse's ass .' He picked up the phone and started calling around.

At 10:45 a.m. Tommy Nowak stepped into the office. 'Knew you'd find me,' he said.

'Wasn't hard,' Buddy said. 'I figured there were only three places you could be at ten in the morning – sparring down at Angelo's gym, drinkin' at Chuck's or in the sack with some bored housewife. And as long as it was one of the first two I'd find you. Now sit down and let me tell you what an idiot I've been.'

'A pleasure.' Tommy sat in a chair across from Buddy's desk, and the bail bondsman proceeded to tell him the story of Lou Ann McGuinn, mother, housewife, and fugitive. He finished by taking the Polaroid out and tossing it across the desk. Tommy picked it up and studied it carefully.

'Obviously a hardcore criminal,' Tommy said. 'The pigtail's a dead giveaway.'

'Look,' Buddy replied. 'She's walked on a bond of twenty-five Gs and as far as I'm concerned she's a fugitive, pigtail or no pigtail. You want her, you don't want her, for me is el same-same.'

'I want her,' Tommy said, glancing at the picture again. 'Any priors?'

'Her old man's the one with the priors,' Buddy answered. 'But I didn't post bond for her old man.'

'You figure they're running together?'

'Nope.' Buddy shook his head. 'In fact, you might get some competition from him. She's probably more scared of her hubby than she is of the law.'

Tommy looked up at him and scowled. 'Why's that?'

Buddy realized he'd said too much. 'Aw, nothing really. It's just that her husband's tied in with a . . . a gang of sorts.'

Tommy smiled. He smelled something fishy. 'What kind of gang, Buddy?'

'Oh, just a gang kind of gang. Buncha ex-cons.'

'Stop shittin' me, Buddy,' Tommy said.

'Well, they call themselves the Birthright.'

Tommy flipped the photo back across the desk and stood up. It was still early and he felt like he could get back in the ring and go another five or six rounds. He was just turning to leave when Buddy grabbed his arm.

'Nope,' Tommy said. 'No, no, no. Try to understand me, Buddy: the rhythmic motion of my lips is me saying, "No, thank you, I do not want this job." '

'But I need you!' Buddy wailed. 'You know what I was saying about you today? I said "Tommy Nowak, I swear that man could track down a shadow in the dead of night." '

'Listen,' Tommy said as he tried to peel Buddy's pudgy fingers off his T-shirt. 'I track fugitives. My job is to produce warm bodies in court. I'm not taking on a bunch of whacked-out ex-cons with automatic weapons.'

Buddy picked up the photo again and pointed at Jasper, smiling in Lou Ann's arms. 'Listen for a minute, Tom. She's a brand new mother, she's never done a thing wrong in her life. She just happened to be in the trailer when the Feds showed up, and she thinks she has to either take the fall or get killed. But you want to know what those Birthright guys are thinking? I guarantee you they're thinking, hey, we better waste her *before* she turns state's evidence. That's right. They have to be figuring she might change her mind and point a finger.'

'So?' Tommy said.

'So I really think you could serve the cause of justice here, Tom.'

Tommy laughed. He couldn't help it. Hearing the word 'justice' come from Buddy's lips was like a hooker talking about the joys of virginity. Buddy looked like he was trying his best to act offended.

'What?' he asked. 'What's so funny? I happen to love our legal system.'

46

'Sure,' Tommy chuckled. 'As long as it keeps you in diamond rings and Sonys.'

Buddy dropped the Polaroid into Tommy's hands. 'Come on, Tom, look at her. Look at that little baby. You wanna see 'em get wasted by those lunatics? Think of it this way. You'd really be saving her by catching her.'

Tommy looked again at the photo. Damn it, he thought. It was the Boy Scout in him. Goddamn it all to hell. If he didn't take the job and those Birthright loonies wound up wasting her he'd never be able to forgive himself.

'OK,' he said, sitting down again. 'Let me see everything you've got on her.'

Ten minutes later he was ready to go. Buddy followed him out to the sidewalk and watched him get into the Fury.

'Where do you think you'll start lookin'?' he asked.

'Out near Reno,' Tommy said.

'Reno?' A pained expression came across Buddy's face. 'Well, watch the mileage, would you?'

Tommy rolled his eyes and started the Fury up, but before he could take off, Buddy leaned in through the passenger window.

'Listen,' the bail bondsman said. 'Do me a favour.'

'What's that?' Tommy asked.

'Try to stay clear of the Birthright, OK?' Buddy said. 'I'd like to use you again some time.'

Lou Ann opened her eyes and found herself staring at a chrome console. What the . . .? Oh, my God, it's real, she thought. For a moment there she'd assumed it was a dream. The whole thing – the counterfeit money, the Secret Service, the courtroom, that bail bondsman, her taking the Cadillac . . . it was hard to believe it was real, that she'd really done it. Lou Ann pushed herself up. The inside of the car was warm and moist, and the windows were slightly fogged. She reached for the door handle and pushed it open. Her legs were stiff from being curled up in the car all night, and she stepped outside to stretch. The air was warm and tasted good. She tugged out the bottom of her T-shirt to let in some fresh air against her skin.

And then she started to laugh at the craziness of it all. It was a laugh of exhilaration, but also of nervousness and fear. Oh, boy, she was in it now. There was no turning back. She'd go get Jasper, but what she'd do after that was anyone's guess. One thing was for certain though, she wasn't going back home.

Lou Ann touched her forehead. Her skin felt oily. What she needed more than anything was to wash her face and have a cup of coffee. She went back to the Caddy and bent down to look at herself in the side mirror. What little make-up she still wore was OK, but her hair needed brushing, and the sight of herself made her laugh again.

'You're about the palest thing,' she said out loud, immitating Mr Barton. She glanced at the Caddy's black top. But why stay that way? Why not enjoy it? Just because Roy never touched it didn't mean she couldn't. She got back into the car and released the clamps that held the convertible top down. Then she turned the ignition key, started the engine, and pressed the button that brought the top down. There was a loud grinding sound as if something was wrong, but then the top rose and started to fold back like an accordian. Just for the hell of it she brought down the windows too. There, that was the way this boat should sail. Not all bundled up like a little old lady, but stripped down like a sexy broad. Lou Ann shook her hair out and slipped on a pair of sunglasses to cut the morning glare. She was going to see her son today, and nothing could be finer.

She'd been on the road maybe fifteen minutes, the wind blowing her hair around and the radio turned up loud, when she found herself behind a yellow school bus. The kids in the back noticed her, and like all kids, they started to make faces and wave. They might have been a little more excited than Lou Ann would have expected, but then she assumed it wasn't everyday they saw a 1959 pink convertible Caddy.

Lou Ann pulled out a little to take a peek around the school bus. God, she hated to pass, but the bus was so slow and she was awful eager to see Jasper. Looking past the bus she didn't see a single car on the long ribbon of highway heading east. Well, she thought, it is certainly a time in your life for trying new things, so she pushed down on the accelerator and began to pass.

Funny thing, even as she started to pass, the kids in the bus were going crazy, pointing, shouting, waving like mad. Lou Ann gripped the steering wheel nervously. What could it be? Lou Ann wondered. After one little boy was particularly vehement about pointing behind her, she glanced up into the rear-view mirror. What the . . .?

Lou Ann slammed on the brakes and the Caddy skidded to a stop. Behind her, fluttering in the air like confetti, were hundreds of green pieces of paper that looked remarkably like US currency. She could tell that it had all been coming from the back of the Cadillac, from the well where the convertible top went. Lou Ann climbed into the back seat. Jammed in one side of the well was a torn brown bag filled with money. Counterfeit no doubt. She looked back down the empty highway, flecked with green for as far as she could see. Well, she couldn't just leave it there for the police or Roy's friends to find. Lou Ann pulled the bag out of the well and threw it in the trunk and then started to walk back down the highway, picking up the bills. She hated to say it, but Jasper would just have to wait.

The camp was a cluster of old, grey wooden out-buildings on a slope near the top of a tall Sierra foothill. The land around it was rugged, craggy, thick with tall pines and fir trees, and scattered boulders. Elk, deer, antelope and wild mustangs roamed these parts. Hawks and eagles circled high overhead on the thermals sweeping off the snowcapped mountains to the east. Some logging had been done in the area many years before, and the logging roads were still intact. But the buildings in the camp had been abandoned for so long, no one could remember why they'd originally been built. Except for the pick-ups and motorcycles parked here and there among the buildings, the place still looked deserted.

By the time Roy and Murray came bouncing up the road they were totally wired. They'd stopped at another liquor store a few hours back for some wine, and later Murray, generous soul that he was, had finally agreed to share some crystal. The combination burned like nitro.

'Speed and wine!' Murray shouted as the pick-up bucked and heaved along the rocky, pockmarked logging road. 'Speed and wine!'

'Yeah!' hooted Roy, who was so stoned he'd temporarily forgotten the fix he was in. 'I want that stuff that killed Hank Williams. I just don't want quite as much!'

They pulled into the camp and stopped. The sudden silence around them was eerie.

'Where are they?' Roy asked.

'Shh.' Murray put his finger to his lips.

Although it wasn't easy, Roy tried to be quiet and still. *Rat-tat-tat-tat-tat!* Even though it was inside one of the buildings, the sudden burst of automatic weapons fire made him flinch.

'Silhouette City,' Murray said and got out of the truck.

'Oh, boy!' Roy grinned. 'Let's go!'

They entered the largest of the outbuildings, a place nearly the size of a barn. The inside was dark, like a fun house. The acrid smell of gunpowder hung in the air. As Roy's eyes adjusted, the 'city' became visible – a small but life-size, three-dimensional town built by hand and painstakingly painted. There was an intersection with a bank and an armoured car parked outside. A gun shop and a drug store were on the opposite side. Silhouettes of life-sized people inhabited this town, but unlike the silhouettes in regular target ranges, these all had real photographs for faces and were dressed in real clothes and uniforms.

A man with short blond hair stepped out of the dark followed by half a dozen others. He was wearing ear protectors, a denim vest over a T-shirt, and chinos. In his hands was a converted MAC-10 automatic rifle. His name was Alex, and he was the leader of the Birthright.

'Yo, Alex!' Roy shouted giddily, raising his hand for a high-five.

Alex stared at him and hardly reacted. Roy suddenly felt the weight of the others' stares as well. They already knew. Roy felt his skin begin to crawl.

'What are you yelling for, Roy?' Alex asked quietly. 'Do you really feel you've earned the right to have a good time?'

'No,' Roy replied meekly. He felt like he was in the sixth grade again, being scolded by the teacher for dropping the ant farm.

Alex turned and let a burst go at a silhouette near the drug store. The target jumped and spun around. As Roy focused on it, he felt a shiver run down his spine. It was a silhouette of a young woman. The photo on the silhouette looked disturbingly familiar. In fact, it looked just . . . like Lou Ann. Alex turned back to Roy.

'What is your problem, Roy?'

Roy swallowed. 'No problem, Alex.'

'Say sir, dickhead!'

'Uh, sir, dickhead!'

The men standing around Alex started to laugh. The Birthright leader shook his head. 'No, you can't be that stupid.'

'Yes, sir,' Roy gulped.

'So tell me, Roy,' Alex said. 'Tell me what's bothering you.' He had this way of looking at you. This intensity. Roy couldn't look him in the eyes.

'I don't . . .' he stammered. 'I, uh, don't like seeing . . .'

The next thing he knew, Alex grabbed his face and started making his mouth move as if he was a dummy or something. Roy let him, too terrified to resist.

'I don't like seeing Lou Ann out there in Silhouette City,' Alex mimmicked, moving Roy's jaw as if he were saying it. The others laughed. Alex let go of Roy's face. 'Don't I always know what you're thinking, Roy?'

Humiliated, rubbing his jaw where Alex had grabbed him, Roy nodded. Alex smiled, then suddenly nudged him towards the target range. 'Go take it down, Roy. Go ahead.'

Roy stepped tentatively into the target-range city. His mind was still numb on speed and booze, but he was alert enough to know that Alex could shoot him and bury him out there in the brush and no one would ever know. Hadn't he seen him do it already to that hitch-hiker Billy Dunston had brought up to the camp a few weeks before? Nice enough kid, but Alex had somehow gotten it into his head that the kid was a liberal. Roy never did quite understand why. The kid sure didn't *look* like a liberal. But the next thing he knew there was gunfire, and the kid was gone. The following morning there were two shovels caked with fresh dirt in the back of Billy's Jeep.

Roy had almost reached Lou Ann's silhouette when he heard Alex shout, 'Stop!'

Roy stopped.

'Turn around,' Alex commanded.

Roy turned slowly. He was trembling. Oh, God, don't let this

51

happen, he prayed. I know I'm a fuck up and a fool, but don't let me go down just yet. He stared back at the dark form of Alex and the others.

'Do you trust me, Roy?' Alex asked ominously.

'Yes, sir, I do,' Roy replied, although the truth was, he wasn't really sure.

'Stand in your wife's silhouette,' Alex ordered.

Roy heard him very clearly, but wished he hadn't. 'Uh, pardon?'

'You heard me,' Alex snarled.

Roy, nervous and confused, began to inch slowly in front of the target. It was weird how Alex never raised his voice, but by simply modifying it, he could make it have the same impact as if he were screaming at the top of his lungs. Roy stopped in front of the target. Twenty-five feet away, Alex lowered the MAC-10 to his hips and aimed. Roy couldn't believe his eyes. He opened his mouth to speak, but his throat was so tight no words came out. Suddenly the barrel of the automatic rifle lit up and the room filled with loud bursts of gunfire. Roy could've sworn he could hear the bullets whiz past his ears. He was seized with such fright that his knees buckled. Then, mercifully the gunfire ended, and in the silence that immediately followed, Roy collapsed on the ground.

The others were laughing. Murray and Billy Dunston gave each other high-fives. Roy's heart was pounding like a jackhammer. He was petrified. He managed to get to his knees, but rose no further. Alex was coming toward him.

'Come on, Roy,' he said, helping him up.

Roy rose uncertainly, wondering what Alex had in store for him next.

'Now here's the point,' Alex said, patting him on the shoulder. 'I need at least a dozen more MAC-10s to build the arsenal of my dreams . . . of our dreams. But our weapons budget, our communications budget, just about our whole fucking budget is riding around in the desert *with your wife*. Now are you man enough to go and get it back?'

Roy's jaw was quivering uncontrollably, but he managed to say, 'Yes, sir.'

'I thought so,' Alex said. He turned and pointed at Murray. 'Waycross, you go with him.'

'Fuckin' A!' Murray said gleefully. 'I am psyched for it! I am ready! Uh, but what do you want me to do about, uh . . .'

'The female?' Alex said. 'Use your best judgement.'

It took hours to collect all the money, and thank God there was no wind. Lou Ann spent about two thirds of the time actually picking up the bills . . . from the roadway, the road shoulder and the brush near the highway. The rest of the time was spent convincing a very excited Mexican woman and her teenaged daughter in an old Volkswagon bus that the $5,000 they'd found was not theirs, finders keepers or otherwise, and that if they did not hand it over she, Lou Ann would have no choice but to call the police and report their licence-plate number as well as the fact that she was certain they were illegal aliens. The woman and her daughter finally agreed to return the money, minus a small labour charge of approximately $500 they claimed they should keep for picking the bills up in the first place. Lou Ann was too aggravated to argue, so she let them have it. The police were going to be pretty damn amused with their explanation when they got picked up for passing counterfeit bills.

It was nearly dinner time when she reached Dinah's house in Carson City. She parked the Caddy in the driveway, pulled the bag of money out of the trunk and rushed to the door.

Dinah pulled it open before Lou Ann could knock, and the two sisters embraced. While they loved each other, their relationship had always been a bit strained. Dinah was the older and more responsible one. Also the plumper and less attractive one. In her teens she had resented Lou Ann's looks and popularity. Later it would be Lou Ann's turn to be jealous when Dinah married Jeff Kugel. He might not've been the world's richest or most ambitious locksmith, but he was a kind and generous man and he was devoted to Dinah in a way that Roy had never been to Lou Ann.

'Oh, hon, it's so good to see you,' Dinah said.

'You too,' said Lou Ann, pulling back from the embrace. 'Is Jasper all right?'

'Sure,' Dinah said. 'I just put him down for a nap, but I know you want to see him.' She led Lou Ann into the bedroom, where Jasper lay on the bed, surrounded on all sides by pillows so he wouldn't roll off and hurt himself. Lou Ann felt such a pang when

53

she saw him sleeping there, his little eyes closed and his little hand clutching a pacifier. It was hard not to scoop him up in her arms.

'I know it's tempting,' Dinah whispered, pulling Lou Ann out of the room and closing the door. 'But he had a rough night. I think you better let him sleep.'

Lou Ann nodded sadly and let herself be led back to the kitchen. By now Dinah had noticed the bag.

'My Lord, you didn't have to bring anything, hon,' she said. 'What with all you've got on your mind already.'

'Look inside,' Lou Ann said. 'You won't believe it.'

Dinah looked in the bag and gasped. 'My *Goodness!* Where did you get this!?'

'It's a long story,' Lou Ann said, reaching into the bag and pulling out some bills. 'And it's all counterfeit anyway. Here, have some.'

Dinah stared at the bills. 'How can you tell they're counterfeit?'

'Oh, you know,' Lou Ann said. 'They put it under one of those little purple lights and it does the wrong thing.'

'Uh huh,' Dinah looked a little puzzled, and she backed away from the money. 'Well, Jeff should be home any minute now. I bet you're starved.'

'That I am,' Lou Ann said.

A little while later Jeff came in and they sat down for a chicken casserole dinner with broccoli and potatoes. By the time they finished, Lou Ann couldn't stand it any longer and went to get Jasper. She brought him back to the living room, where Jeff sat, taking the money out of the bag and making stacks. He'd once done a stint as a cashier over at Harrah's in Tahoe and had learned to estimate amounts simply by looking at the stuff.

Lou Ann sat down on the couch and hugged and kissed Jasper, who yawned and cried a little at being awakened. Dinah beamed as her sister played with her little boy, but soon their attention turned back to the money, as if they were mesmerized by it, even if it was counterfeit.

Lou Ann gave one of the bills to Jasper and let him gum it. 'Man, just think if that cash was genuine I'd have his Harvard tuition all paid for already.'

'I figure there's about two hundred and fifty thousand there,' Jeff said. 'Harvard? Yep, that'd just about do it.'

Dinah picked up another bill and squinted at it. 'I dunno, hon. It sure looks real. Strange to think it's just a baby's toy.'

They stared at the money a while longer and then Jeff went into the bedroom and came back with a canvas money sack like the ones the banks and Wells Fargo used.

'Here's a little souvenir from my cashier's days,' he said. 'I think you better keep the money in it, Lou Ann. That way you won't find it fluttering out over the highway again.'

He began to pack the money back into the bag. He and Dinah were casting funny glances at each other and Lou Ann started to get the feeling something was going on.

'Hey, what is it?' she asked.

Jeff and Dinah gave each other a long look. Then Dinah turned to her.

'Look, hon. Jeff and I were talking while you were in the bedroom with the baby. We think you ought to cut loose for a bit. Take this play money and go have a weekend on the town in Reno.'

'What?' Lou Ann was kind of stunned. 'But I just got here.'

'We know, Lou,' Jeff said. 'But the thing of it is, you're a fugitive. We figured, uh, just in case anybody comes after you . . . Like, you got to believe this would be their first stop. It's only logical.'

'You mean, leave Jasper *again?*' Lou Ann asked.

Jeff nodded. Lou Ann saw his point, but she couldn't stand the idea of giving up her son again. She turned and stared at Dinah.

'We'd all better scatter for a few days, hon,' her sister said. 'Give this thing a little time to blow over.'

'We'll take the baby over to my folks' house,' Jeff said. 'He'll be safe there.'

Lou Ann blinked to fight back the tears. She'd risked so much and come all this way to see her son, and now they were telling her to leave him again. She guessed it made sense, but it was so darn hard. And there was another problem.

'But the money's counterfeit,' she said.

'Listen,' Jeff said. 'I know casinos have those bad bill detectors, but I can tell you that in all the time I worked over in Tahoe, we only used it once, and that was on a bill so obvious you would've thought a five-year-old drew it. Truth is they don't have time to check every goddarn bill that comes through and never will. The dealers are supposed to take a look at it when you buy chips, but they see a million bills a day and after a while they're strickly on autopilot. This here's high quality stuff, Lou Ann. Ain't a dealer in all of Reno's gonna notice, or a cashier who's gonna bother to check. You go on over to the Bally Grand and enjoy yourself for a few days. By then we'll know whether anyone's lookin' for you or not.'

Dinah patted her on the shoulder. 'And get a little sun while you're at it.'

A little while later Lou Ann was back in the Cadillac heading north on 395 toward Reno. The sack of money was in the well behind the backseat. She wasn't happy, but, she told herself, if staying away for a few more days would help ensure her safety, then for Jasper's sake, she would do it. After all, what was a few days when they had another twenty years together?

On the outskirts of Reno she saw a big store all lit up. The sign said, 'BUSTER'S DEPT. STORE – OPEN ALL NIGHT.' Lou Ann knew immediately that Buster's was no tourist trap. The reason it was open all night was to catch the dealers and casino workers who got off their late shifts and were too wired to go directly to bed. Lou Ann decided to stop. If Jeff was right about the money, then there were some things she wanted to get.

Half an hour later she was carrying an armload of expensive children's clothes down the aisle towards the cashier. She had to admit that picking them out had been fun. What a wonderful feeling it was to have enough money to buy whatever she wanted without even having to think about what it cost!

At the cash register she began to lay out all the outfits, sweaters, sleepers, and underwear on the counter. The cashier, a young woman, started ringing it all up, and as she did, she kept giving Lou Ann the oddest looks. For a second Lou Ann felt a fright. Did the cashier recognize her? Was there some kind of wanted poster out for her? Then she realized what it was. The cashier was looking at *her clothes*. Lou Ann looked down at her T-shirt and jeans. Pretty shabby when you compared it to what she was buying for Jasper. She looked up and the cashier smiled at her.

'Bet you read my mind,' she said.

'I do look a little raggedy, don't I?' Lou Ann asked.

'Well, it looks like you must've had a pretty good night at the tables,' the cashier said. 'I mean, why not treat yourself to something new too, right? You don't want your baby looking more glamorous than you, do you?'

Lou Ann smiled. 'Well . . . maybe just one dress.'

5

It was late when Tommy got to the small ranch house in Carson City. The Cadillac wasn't there, but that didn't mean anything. If she was smart, she would've sold the damn thing or dumped it. He parked the Fury across the street and slowly walked up the lawn through the dark. In the driveway he noticed a big oil stain. That meant a car was usually parked there. So where was it? Tommy stepped quietly up to the garage and took a tiny flashlight out of his pocket. Flicking it on, he peered in the garage window. There was a boat in there but no Cadillac.

Tommy was cautious. No cars usually meant no one was home, but it could have been a trick just to make it look that way. He quietly walked around to the back of the house and stood for a long time under the open bedroom window, listening for a snore, a groan, the rustling of sheet. Some sixth sense told him no one was there. Finally he peeked up and shined the flashlight through a crack in the curtains. He could see some pillows laid out in a circle on the bed, but no one was sleeping there.

It took him about twenty seconds to card the back door and he was in. In the kitchen he found three dinner plates and three glasses drying in the dish rack. The oven still felt warm. In the bathroom garbage was an empty canister of baby wipes. Finally, on the living-room couch, half chewed and crumpled up into a ball, was a twenty-dollar bill.

Tommy let himself out of the house and got back into the Fury. He was on the right track, and it felt good. Truth was, Tommy was never happier than when he was on the trail. Had he been born a hundred years earlier, he would've been an Indian tracker or some kind of scout. He'd gone to Nam knowing he'd be the point man, always out in the jungle fifty yards ahead of his platoon. Sure it was sixty times more dangerous than staying back with the group, but there had never been any doubt, that was simply where he had to be.

On the way up 395 to Reno, he stopped at a gas station/convenience store for coffee and fuel. It was a mild night and some bugs and moths swarmed in the overhead lights. He stretched and sipped the coffee, waiting for the pump attendant to finish filling the Fury. When the tank was full he peeled off a couple of bills. As the attendant gave him the change, Tommy had a thought.

'You seen a blonde in a pink Cadillac?' he asked.

The pump attendant thought about it for a moment. 'Only in my dreams, Mister.'

Roy McGuinn was starting to hallucinate. It wasn't acid, it was crystal, booze and lack of sleep. Coming down out of the mountains with Murray, who hadn't slept in days either, he could've sworn it was snowing, but then he'd shaken it off and realized it was a sunny day. The weird thing was, Murray had the windshield wipers on.

'You won't believe this,' he told Murray. 'But a second ago I hallucinated a snowstorm.'

'Shit no, can't you see it's pouring rain?' Murray replied.

Roy squinted at the windshield. The wipers had cut clean swarths through the dust. There wasn't a drop of rain on them. 'I think it's stopped,' he said.

Murray frowned and stuck his hand out the window. A moment later he pulled it in and showed it to Roy. 'If it's stopped, what do you call this?'

Roy stared down and tried to focus on Murray's hand. There wasn't a single drop of rain there, either.

'I call it a hand, Murray.'

'Huh?' Murray started down at his hand. 'Jesus shit, you're right!'

'Right that it's a hand? Or right that it's not raining?' Roy asked.

Murray didn't respond, but he did turn off the windshield wipers. Roy slumped down in the seat and sighed. There they were, all fucked up and everyplace to go.

Their first stop was back to the campground to see if Lou Ann had doubled back that way. Murray parked outside the manager's office and they went in. Mr Barton was in there, sitting in one of those dumb chairs made out of branches, watching some TV game show. When he saw Murray and Roy come in he got this look in his face. Sort of like fear.

'You seen Lou?' Roy asked.

'Un, no I ain't, Roy,' Mr Barton said. He started to get up.

'Where're you goin' old boy?' Murray asked.

'Well, I was uh, just goin' in the back here, that's all.' Mr Barton was trembling. It sort of made Roy feel good to think that just his very presence struck fear in the hearts of men. Sort of like the Incredible Hulk or something.

'You sure you ain't seen his wife?' Murray asked the older man.

'Like I said, no sir,' Mr Barton repeated. 'I ain't seen hide or hair of her since the day she—'

Before he could finish, Murray let loose a backhanded smash to Mr Barton's face that knocked him clear against the wall and down on to the floor. Roy was aghast.

'Jesus Christ, man, he doesn't know,' he said. 'You didn't have to do that.'

Murray was rubbing the back of his hand and grinning maniacally. 'It's true I didn't *have* to. But I try to live for the moment, Roy my boy. What can I stay? I'm a spontaneous person.'

Murray headed out the door and got back into the truck. Roy followed, but he was starting to have serious doubts.

Tommy found the Cadillac in the parking lot of the Bally Grand, just sitting there plain as day. He could hardly believe his eyes. Either this skip desperately wanted to be caught or she was the senior space cadet of the year. Either way, he parked the Fury nearby.

The casino was buzzing. It was the size of a football field and crowded with gamblers betting against the odds. In a small amphitheatre directly in front of him, tired people lounged in padded seats watching the keno wheel. To their left came ratchet sounds and clangs from the banks of slot machines. Beyond that, dozens of men crowded around the craps tables, occasionally shouting and hooting with joy. And then there were the endless blackjack tables, the slapping of cards and calculations of the dealers lost in the din.

Tommy tried the slot machines first, usually the bastion of old ladies and novice gamblers too timid to try the tables. Was that chauvinistic? No, realistic. It was late and he was getting low on patience. When it came right down to it, he just wanted to grab Lou Ann McGuinn and get back to Sacramento. He roamed the aisles of slot machines, past the old ladies mindlessly yanking the metal arms down, dipping into their paper cups filled with silver dollars whenever they ran low. He soon noticed he wasn't the only one roaming. A greasy-haired lounge lizard wearing a slightly wrinkled beige suit was checking the silver machine basins where the coins fell. Some of the old ladies were so blind they sometimes left behind a few silver coins when they won, and the lounge lizard obviously hoped to find enough to score a drink.

But Lou Ann McGuinn wasn't there. Tommy took out the Polaroid and glanced at it again. Well, if she wasn't doing the slots she could be anywhere. He wandered over to the section of the casino reserved for high rollers. This area, slightly elevated and tucked away in a corner, had the quiet, reserved air of a high-priced restaurant. A lone player with a huge, gold pinky ring played black jack, and several well-dressed men and women sat at the baccarat table. One of the women was a blonde. Tommy took out the photo again.

'May I help you?' a haughty voice asked.

Tommy looked up at a man in a tuxedo. He had slicked, black hair and a diamond stud in his ear. The look he gave Tommy made him feel like he had maggots crawling around his body. Why? Tommy wondered. Just because he's wearing some cheap tux and I'm in a T-shirt? Well, screw him.

'Sir?' the host repeated.

'Yeah,' Tommy said rubbing his neck. 'My neck is cramped up and I was wondering if you could massage it for me?'

The host's jaw dropped. Tommy laughed and slapped him playfully on the back, saying, 'Naw, thanks anyhow, another time maybe.'

The host gawked at him. Tommy checked the blonde at the baccarat table, but she wasn't the one.

At that moment Lou Ann sat fifty feet away at a blackjack table watching the dealer cut and shuffle the cards. The man to her right smiled at her. Several more men were standing behind her for no

61

real purpose other than to gaze at her and watch her play. Lou Ann glanced up at the mirrored ceiling, knowing that on the other side of that mirror was a camera, monitoring the action at the tables. She didn't care. What she saw was a stunning woman in a slinky red off-the-shoulder dress staring back down at her. The woman's hair was done up like an heiress's, like those women in *Vogue*. From her ears dangled long red earrings. Lou Ann smiled. The woman, of course, was her.

The dealer shuffled and glanced at her. At the edge of the table in front of Lou Ann was one last green $25 chip. She figured she'd gone through close to a $1,000 worth of the counterfeit money in the last hour. This, she was certain, interested the other players and lounge lizards as much as her new looks. She wondered what they'd say if they knew she was only pretending. In a way she felt as counterfeit as the bills she'd purchased the chips with. They all looked impressed. It must've appeared to them that she'd gone through the money without blinking an eye. It wasn't hard when it wasn't real. In fact, it was almost fun. And maybe, after all she'd been through, she deserved some fun.

The dealer finished shuffling and slid the tall stack of cards into the shoe. Lou Ann put up the last $25 chip. The dealer burned the first card off the shoe and started to deal. Lou Ann got a king and a six. Unless the dealer showed some garbage she was going to have to hit. Behind her one of the lounge lizards moved a little closer.

'Your skin,' he whispered in her ear. His breath was like a fog of booze.

'Please do not talk to the players while a hand is in progress,' the dealer said, flipping a king as his up card.

Damn, Lou Ann thought. 'Hit me.'

The dealer slid an eight out of the shoe. She'd busted. Behind her the lounge lizard whispered. 'It's so soft, like . . . Velveeta. You know Velveeta?'

Lou Ann stiffened. She'd lost her last $25 chip. It was time to get away. She turned and faced him.

'That's very sweet,' she said sarcastically. 'My flesh reminds you of processed cheese.'

Ten feet away Tommy had watched the whole thing. He kept looking at the woman in the Polaroid and this gorgeous creature at the blackjack table. Somehow he knew they were one and the same, but it wasn't easy to believe. Now she was on the move and he had his shot. Moving quickly past the lounge lizards, he touched her lightly on the arm.

'Lou Ann McGuinn?' he whispered, getting a breathful of perfume. 'I'd like to have a word with you for a moment.'

Lou Ann felt a chill run through her, and her shoulders slumped down. She didn't even have to look at him. He knew her name and that was that. Fun while it lasted, she supposed. Deep inside she'd known all along it was going to have to end.

He led her into a darkened lounge where a middle-aged man and woman in matching baby-blue satin outfits were entertaining the empty tables and booths. Tommy guided her to a table in the back and for the first time she glanced at him. Not at all what she expected. He was lean and hard, and despite the stubble on his chin, the old T-shirt and denim jacket, he was a hell of a lot better-looking than any other man who'd touched her arm in recent years. He slumped down a little in the cushiony seat and didn't seem at all in a rush. On the stage the female half of the duo, who was about fifty and wore bright-blue eye make-up to match her outfit, addressed them: 'Ladies and gentlemen. Bill and I would like to offer our tribute to a bunch of guys we like to call the greatest rock and roll band in the world. Now you know that's gotta be none other than the incredible Rolling Stones!'

The next thing Lou Ann knew, they broke into a duet of 'Some Girls', and started dancing around the stage like a geriatric Fred Astaire and Ginger Rogers. This can't be real, she thought. But then again, stranger things had and were happening. She glanced again at the guy sitting with her. He was staring at the entertainers too. Sure didn't seem to be in any kind of a rush. Lou Ann opened her bag and took out a cigarette.

Tommy picked up a pack of casino matches lying in the ashtray and lit the cigarette for her. She looked real pretty in the match light. Too bad he had to take her in.

'Looks like somebody gave you some real nice stuff recently,' he said, taking out the Polaroid and sliding it across the table to her. 'Recognize this woman?'

Lou Ann looked down at the photo. It was the one she'd given that fat bail bondsman, Donovan.

'She looks vaguely familiar,' Lou Ann replied, almost sadly.

'Like someone who never really caught a break. Someone who might just go stone crazy for a day.'

She handed the picture back to Tommy. 'You're a cop, right?'

'Not exactly,' Tommy replied.

'What do you mean, "not exactly"?' Lou Ann asked.

'I'm a skip tracer, Mrs McGuinn,' Tommy said, taking out his state-issued ID and showing it to her. 'I work for Buddy Donovan, the bondsman who posted your bail. My job's to bring you back.'

Lou Ann nodded and looked down regretfully at her pretty red dress. She hated to see the night end like this. She'd hardly even worn it yet.

'Uh, just out of curiosity, Mrs McGuinn,' Tommy said. 'I sort of heard your story. Why didn't you just let your husband's friends put up the money?'

Lou Ann felt herself stiffen. That wasn't his business. She cruched out her cigarette and picked up her purse. The skip tracer looked surprised.

'Look,' Lou Ann said. 'If you're taking me back, we might as well get started—' she gestured to the middle-aged duo on the small stage – 'I don't think I could get through their tribute to Elvis.'

Tommy was impressed. He liked a woman, or a man for that matter, who showed grace under pressure. As she rose from her seat, he instinctively got up and pulled her chair out for her. Together they left the lounge and started back across the casino floor. Tommy looked down and noticed that she was wearing high heels. It was sort of amusing to see how she turned the heads of the gamblers and lounge lizards.

'I know it ain't my place to say this,' he said. 'But you sure are dressed to kill this evening.'

'No, I'm dressed to torture,' Lou Ann replied with a faint smile and a glance at her admirers. 'Killing's too good for them.'

Tommy chuckled and led her towards the doors. Lou Ann noticed that the drunken lounge lizard who'd paid her the Velveeta compliment was following them. He looked angry and disappointed, as if he somehow thought Lou Ann had chosen the skip tracer over him. She glanced at Tommy. He certainly did look strong and fast, but lately she'd learned that appearances could be deceiving. An impulsive thought struck her. Maybe the night was still young after all.

They were just at the doors when she suddenly shoved him out of the way and took off, her heels scraping noisily across the marble floor as she pushed through the doors and headed for the parking lot. As Tommy got to his feet he marvelled at how fast she was in those shoes. Fast, but, of course, not fast enough.

He was just about to go through the doors himself when the lounge lizard blind-sided him with a full body block. They both went flying, sliding across the polished floor, flopping and grappling like a couple of polar bears on a sheet of ice.

'Hey, wait a second!' Tommy shouted as he struggled out of the lounge lizard's grip and tried to get up. 'I got a warrant for that woman.'

'Oh, that's a good one!' the lounge lizard laughed, catching Tommy by the ankles and tripping him again.

Tommy got to his knees. Goddamn it, he thought. She was gonna get away. The damn lounge lizard was crawling up his back and Tommy spun around, smacked him one across the head and then gave him a knee his stomach would remember for the rest of its life. He jumped up and ran for the doors. He could see Mrs McGuinn out in the parking lot now, pulling the Caddy's door open.

There was just no point in giving in to these men so easily, Lou Ann was thinking as she started up the Cadillac and backed out of her parking place. After all, what made them think they were God's gift to anything? With renewed confidence, she got the Caddy straightened out and headed for the exit.

But before she could get there, that skip tracer came out of the hotel and stood in the middle of the road. God, the nerve of him, just standing there in front of the car like he was so damn certain she wouldn't run him over.

Lou Ann hit the brakes. You couldn't kill someone just to prove a point. Well, at least she couldn't. Through the windshield she could see that the skip tracer wasn't gloating over his triumph. He just wanted her to stop. Lou Ann sighed. One escape attempt was all she had in her at the moment. She was just getting out of the Cadillac when the lounge lizard came running out of the casino, puffing and staggering under the parking lot lights.

'You OK?' he gasped, pointing at the skip tracer. 'Want me to take care of this guy?'

Lou Ann smiled. It didn't look like he'd done a very good job so far. 'It's all right,' she said. 'Thanks anyway.'

The lounge lizard stared at Lou Ann and Tommy, a confused look on his face. Tommy shrugged and led Lou Ann towards the Fury.

'I didn't think a woman could move so fast in stiletto heels,' he said.

'I took special lessons from Tina Turner,' Lou Ann replied.

Tommy didn't want to put her in the cage. It was true that she'd shown an inclination towards evasive action, but the cage was really for potentially violent types, and while she'd given him a pretty good shove back there in the casino, he didn't think she'd cause him any real harm. So instead he let her sit in the front with him. An honour, actually. It was the first time he'd ever invited a skip to do it.

Sitting in the front seat of the Fury, Lou Ann vacillated between trying to find yet another way out of this mess and just resigning herself to the fact that she'd probably never get out of it. She was too weary to try to run again. Not only physically weary, but mentally as well. She felt defeated, realizing that she would probably never be able to escape the fate that awaited her back in Sacramento.

Oddly enough, it was the skip tracer's car that got her mind going again. It was even worse than she'd imagined, all beat up and stinking of stale cigarette smoke and sweat. Not a single gauge on the dashboard appeared to work. In the back, the cage spoke for itself – that was undoubtedly where he usually put his bounty. The squalor of the car made her think about what jail would be like, and thinking of jail made her think of Jasper again. Thinking of Jasper made her want to try anything to stay free.

'Uh, listen, Mr . . . uh,' she began.

'Nowak. Tom Nowak.'

'Listen, Mr Nowak,' Lou Ann said. 'I have an eight-month-old baby and . . .'

'I'm sorry,' he cut her short. 'Don't even go into it. I'm just a delivery boy.'

Lou Ann frowned. Well, that certainly wasn't very nice. Who did he think he was, anyway? Mr Tough Guy?

'Hey,' she said acidly, 'Aren't you going to handcuff me?'

He didn't answer. Now he was ignoring her. God, that made her mad. He should've appreciated the fact that she hadn't tried to claw his eyeballs out with her newly manicured fingernails.

'I just figured that a guy like you would be into handcuffs,' she said, goading him. 'The whole bondage part of the job. Come on, aren't you into that?'

'Bondage, lady?' Tommy glanced at her a moment and then looked back out at the road. 'Hell, I don't even like starch in my collars.'

It was late and dark by the time Roy and Murray found that damn house of Dinah's in Carson City. It shouldn't have taken them so long, but with all that crystal and wine running around in his brain, Roy was having a hard time remembering things. Finally they found it. Murray parked the pick-up in the driveway and pulled his carbine out of the gun rack.

'What're you gonna do with that?' Roy asked nervously.

'Don't worry, I'm just gonna scare 'em,' Murray said. He hopped out of the truck. Roy followed, shoving his hands deep in his pockets and staring at the ground as he walked. Murray stopped near the kitchen window and tried to peek in, but the house was dark. 'Could be a trap,' he mumbled.

'Could also be they're asleep,' Roy said.

Murray hunkered up to the front door commando-style and pressed his ear against it, then stood back. He lifted his leg like a dog and *Wham!* kicked the door open and jumped into the dark living-room.

'Don't anyone move!' he shouted.

Roy followed him in. 'Doesn't look like there's anyone here to move, Murray.'

'Turn on the fuckin' lights,' Murray barked at him. Roy did as he was told. Seemed like ever since Alex had shot at him in Silhouette City he'd been relegated to the position of gofer.

Carbine cocked and ready, Murray moved cautiously down the hallway and kicked the bedroom door open. 'Don't move!' Roy heard him shout again, followed by the lights going on and a disappointed 'Aw, shit.'

A moment later Murray stomped back out of the bedroom. 'Damn it, I sure was lookin' forward to shootin' someone tonight,' he grumbled angrily.

It wasn't like he always stopped and picked up a couple of cold beers on the way back to Sacramento with a skip, but tonight Tommy felt moved to do so, and he gave in to the urge. Sipping the cold brews, they cruised down the noisy main street of Reno, past the glaring neon signs of the downtown casinos, the tacky wedding chapels and the pawn shops. Tommy still couldn't figure Lou Ann McGuinn out. He knew he probably shouldn't even try, but what the hell – there he was and there she was, and it was going to be a long drive home.

'So you didn't want to take bail money from the Birthright,' he said. 'But you didn't mind floating some of their counterfeit bills?'

Lou Ann had to chuckle. 'I guess it does seem a little strange, but I thought I had it all figured out. See, I was gonna take just a teeny little bit of the make-believe money, and with it I was gonna win a whole lot of the real stuff at the tables and leave it for Jasper.'

'Jasper?'

'My son,' Lou Ann said. Then she laughed. 'Some plan, huh? Sounds like one of my husband's great ideas.'

'From what I heard, Roy is tilted sideways a little bit,' Tommy said. He knew he was stepping into dangerous territory, but something was egging him on. 'How'd you wind up with him anyway?'

Lou Ann was surprised to hear the question. She definitely had a feeling he was showing her more interest than he showed the average bail jumper. Ever since he'd cut short her story about Jasper she'd been a little angry. But now it was more like she was angry at the world than at him. Besides, she couldn't deny that he was attractive. But she knew she'd better be careful just the same. She stared straight ahead, looking past the garish lights of Reno as she spoke.

'Well, believe it or not,' she said, 'Roy used to be about the coolest boy in San Bernardino. Of course that was about forty thousand Heinekens ago.'

She paused to take a long pull from the can. The beer was cold and refreshing. It would've been a lovely moment had he not been taking her back to jail.

'I guess I thought I was marrying James Dean or something,' she said with a sigh. 'Instead I wound up with a deadbeat on amphetamines.'

Tommy smiled at her a little. 'You know, I hear that same basic story from a lot of women.'

'I'll bet,' Lou Ann said with a laugh. She felt good despite herself. Cruising with a boy and a beer. It was almost like high school. She turned towards him. 'You know, I've still got two hundred and fifty thousand dollars of very high quality counterfeit cash.'

His reaction surprised her. Suddenly he stiffened and stared at the road, his eyes fixed in a stern glare. 'Forget it. I'd turn it down even if it was real.'

'I didn't mean it that way!' Lou Ann replied defensively.

'Oh, you didn't?' Tommy snorted.

'No, I didn't,' Lou Ann insisted, even though she knew it wasn't quite the truth. She pushed a curly lock of hair away from her face. 'I just thought it might be a lot easier for me if I turned that money over to the cops. I thought may be we could go back and pick it up and . . .'

'No way,' Tom cut her off. 'Helping you with your legal case is absolutely none of my business. My job is just to follow you, find you, and Federal Express you back home.'

'That's why you stopped for a few beers,' Lou Ann said with a smile. 'That's why we're cruising nice and leisurely through Reno when we could've been on the highway already. Come on, Mr Tough Guy, don't you think you're being a little hard on yourself?'

'I don't know what you're talking about,' Tommy insisted uncomfortably.

Lou Ann grew bolder as she watched him shift nervously.

'Let me put it to you this way, Mr Skip *Chaser*,' Lou Ann said. 'You want to know where that money is right now? It's back in that Cadillac. Now maybe I should've told you that before we left the casino, but somehow it just happened to slip my memory.'

'So? Why should I care?' Tommy asked.

'Well, maybe you shouldn't,' Lou Ann said. 'It's just that we both know those boys from the Birthright must be out there looking for it too. Can you imagine what kind of guns and explosives that kind of money could buy?'

Tommy pulled the Fury on to the road shoulder. Damn, she was a tough one. He hated the way she affected him, but she did have a point. Normally he didn't give a damn about this political crap, but something about those Birthright guys just rubbed him the wrong way. All this shit about Blacks and Jews and conspiracies and goin' around blowing stuff up with plastic explosives. They were just a bunch of goddamn speed-freak terrorists pretending to be righteous behind some warped ideology.

'Shit!' Tommy whacked the steering wheel with the palm of his hand. Then he turned around and headed back.

Twenty minutes later he pulled into the parking space next to the Cadillac. Lou Ann started to get out, but he grabbed her wrist.

'Now listen good,' he said, jerking his thumb toward the cage in the back of the Fury. 'You better be tellin' me the truth and you better not be tryin' to pull another fast one, or else you're gonna ride all the way back to Sacramento in that cage, understand?'

Lou Ann raised her free hand. 'Girl Scouts' honour, Mr Skip *Chaser*.'

'It's skip *tracer*.' Tommy let her go and watched her climb into the back seat of the Cadillac. Jesus, women, he thought. Maybe he should have a new policy of going after male fugitives only. With men everything was very clearly defined. They ran, he chased and eventually caught 'em. But women . . . somehow they always managed to cloud the issue.

So where was she anyway? Tommy leaned over and peered into the back of the Caddy. She was in the back seat, trying to pull something out of the well behind it. He felt tired and glanced at his watch. Jesus, at this rate they were never gonna make it back to Sacramento that night.

She was still struggling with the canvas money bag. Tommy was losing all patience. Finally he jumped out of the Fury and headed for the Caddy. 'Man,' he said to himself. 'This is so fucking wrong . . .'

He got in the back seat with her. Lou Ann moved out of the way and let him try to get the sack out. Tommy gave it a yank, but it wouldn't budge. Must've been caught in the machanism somehow.

'See why it made such a good hiding place?' Lou Ann asked proudly.

Tommy answered with a grunt. Of all the goddamn stupid things. Meanwhile Lou Ann stretched out in the back seat and made herself comfortable.

'Kind of reminds you of going to the drive-in movie, doesn't it?' she asked as he struggled with the bag. 'Or parking in the woods, listening to the crickets off in the—'

'Will you please shut up!' Tommy snapped. In his anger he gave the sack one final great yank which pulled it free. The sudden momentum knocked Tommy backwards into the front seat. Lou Ann couldn't help laughing. She got out of the car and pulled the sack behind her. It felt sort of heavy, and she didn't think she could manage it in her high heels. Tommy got out behind her and she glanced at him.

'Uh, could you help me with this?' she asked innocently.

The next thing she knew, the skip tracer exploded. From the way he reacted, you would've thought she'd asked him for the world, her freedom and a $50 loan to boot.

'My God!' he shouted at her, grabbing the sack. 'I don't believe this little-girl-lost routine!'

Then, to her surprise, he started to mimic her: 'Sure I've been indicted for a major felony, but that doesn't mean I'm not feminine. Sometimes I want a man to take control! I guess you could say I'm that *Cosmo* fugitive.'

'All I asked you for was a favour,' Lou Ann huffed with her hands on her hips. 'You don't have to go mocking me. I'm all through taking shit from men.'

'Well, that's one thing we have in common,' Tommy said with a faint smile. 'I'm all through taking shit from men too.'

They stared at each other for a moment and then both cracked up. Here they were, two practically total strangers in the middle of the night, standing between two parked cars holding a canvas bag with a quarter of a million dollars in counterfeit money, bitching at each other like an old married couple. Tommy

71

slumped wearily against the side of the Cadillac and caught his breath. Then he glanced at his watch.

'No way I can make it back to Sacramento in one haul,' he groaned.

They both got quiet for a moment. The air was getting cool and a little moist. The crickets were chirping, and they could hear the distant sand of a coyote yelping in the hills. The Bally Grand was up on a rise outside the city of Reno, and when they looked down at the city they saw that the neon lights were all still flashing. But in the surrounding valley, most of the residential sections were dark. Lou Ann glanced up at the bright lights of the Bally Grand. If they couldn't make it all the way to Sacramento that night, they'd have to stop somewhere along the way. And here they were at a hotel to begin with. She glanced at Tommy and noticed he too was looking at the hotel.

'You thinking what I'm thinking?' she asked.

'Maybe.'

'I mean, what's the point of driving for an hour and then stopping in some fleabag motel when we could get a good night's sleep here?' Lou Ann asked.

He studied her carefully, assuming naturally that she was thinking of escaping. Well, there was no point in trying to second guess her. He'd just have to see what she tried to pull next. In the meantime she was right about the hotel – it sure beat the kinds of places he was used to staying in.

As they walked back in through the front entrance and passed the big marbled mirrors on the walls, Tommy had to admit they made an unusual couple. Mrs McGuinn looked like some glamorous movie star, and he looked like a mechanic with a canvas bag over his shoulder. As they passed the front desk, he noticed the desk clerk staring at him with a bemused smile on his lips.

'Uh, bringing home your winnings, sir?' the clerk asked.

Tommy glanced at Lou Ann and back at the clerk. 'Yeah.'

The clerk also gave Lou Ann a good, long once-over. 'Looks as if the gentleman was very lucky tonight,' he said slyly.

'Actually, I've been been arrested for counterfeiting,' Lou Ann said, irritated by his smug suggestion. 'He's taking me back to jail so he's got to keep me under round-the-clock surveillance.'

The desk clerk grinned and nodded. He'd heard some really good ones in his time, but this had to take the cake.

The wallpaper in Lou Ann's suite was fire-engine red with fuzzy designs of flowers and birds. The bed, a big round canopied affair with a mirror in the ceiling, was on a raised platform in the middle of the room as if it was some sort of stage upon which plays were produced. Considering the number of hookers Lou Ann thought she'd seen that night, it made sense.

While Lou Ann kicked off her heels, Tommy collapsed on the bed and picked up the phone. She went into the bathroom and started taking off her jewellery, leaving the door ajar so that she could listen in on his conversation. She heard him punch in eleven numbers, one for an outside line and ten for a long distance call.

'Hey, Buddy . . . Yeah, I know it's late . . . Look, it's me . . . In Reno . . . No, I haven't found her yet . . .'

Lou Ann stuck her head out of the bathroom and gave him a look. Tommy pressed his finger against his lips and shook his head, then spoke into the phone again.

'Of course I'm close . . . Yeah, yeah she's around, I've got her scent . . . Should pick her up tomorrow, I figure . . . What? Will you shut up about the goddamn mileage . . . I mean it . . . OK, I'll call you tomorrow either way.'

He hung up the phone and shook his head. 'Fucking mileage.'

'Why'd you lie to him?' Lou Ann asked as she stood in the bathroom doorway unhooking her earrings.

'I just didn't want to start explaining things,' Tommy said. He got up, stretched and looked around the room, shaking his head at the gaudiness of it all.

Lou Ann reached over and pulled open the door of the little brown refrigerator against the wall.

'Care for something from our complimentary mini-bar?' she asked as if she were an airline stewardess.

'Yeah, that's the whole idea, right?' Tommy said as he slumped into an imitation Louis XIV armchair. 'Keep the customer just tipsy enough so that he forgets what the real game is. That's the whole point of using chips. It's one step removed from real money. Just far enough so that the gambler forgets what he's actually playing with.'

'I didn't realize you'd done such heavy thinking on the topic,' Lou Ann said.

Tommy chuckled. 'I'll take a taste of the Chivas. But just a taste.' Then he got up and went to the curtains and spread them so that the lights from the parking lot came in. 'And we'll leave this curtain partway open, so it doesn't get too dark in here.'

All this amused Lou Ann. Did he really, think she might try to seduce him? Or maybe he wanted it light so he could keep a better eye on her. She took out one of those airline-sized bottles of Chivas and poured him a drink. Then she went over and handed it to him.

'Are you sure you won't need a chaperone too?' she asked.

Tommy just smirked.

Later Lou Ann lay on the bed, her white T-shirt and panties glowing slightly in the dim light coming through the curtains. She was watching the skip tracer, slumped down and fast asleep in his chair. He'd placed the chair between the bed and the bathroom, so there was no way she could escape, or even get to the bathroom, without stepping over his long legs. As she watched him she thought of Jasper again, and of her life. She'd just allowed herself to be swept away along for the longest time, accepting whatever came, somehow assuming it was what she deserved. She'd always laughed at people who planned and schemed and used phrases like 'make things happen', but now she didn't think it was so funny. You could either make things happen or sit back and accept whatever came. Look where that had got her so far.

Quietly she slid off the bed and tip toed toward him, stepping gently over his legs and—

His hand shot out like a viper and clamped like a vice around her ankle, leaving her trying to balance on one foot.

'Hey, I was just getting some water,' she complained.

'Sure you were,' Tommy said with a laugh.

'I'm serious.'

'So am I,' said Tommy.

They stayed like that for a while, her hopping around trying to balance on one foot, him holding her other leg by the ankle, like it was some weird dance. Maybe, in a funny way it was. Lou Ann was amused by the thought. Finally, her eyes caught his.

'Feel good?' she asked.

6

It was early morning, still kind of grey and cool out. Up on the mesas the rimrock glowed reddish like stirred coals on a dying fire. Roy was beyond worn out. He was *worn-through*. So dog tired it was an effort to raise his hand to rub his weary eyes. His eyeballs felt a little funny, a little hard. As if they were stuffed to the brim with the shit he'd seen. But deep inside he knew he hadn't seen anything like the shit he was about to see. He shuddered at the thought of facing Alex empty-handed. He thought Murray must have felt the same way, because they drove all the way to the Birthright camp in silence.

They rode up the bumpy logging road and pulled into the camp and parked.

'Let me do the talking,' Murray said as they got out.

With pleasure, Roy thought.

They went into the meeting building. Even though it was early, Alex was up at the podium, giving another one of his speeches. The rest of the group sat in the seats like schoolchildren. Roy could tell by their faces that it was the same old shit Alex always talked about. But everyone listened just the same.

As soon as he and Murray came in, Alex stopped talking. Everyone turned and stared at them.

'Well, did you get the female?' Alex asked.

Murray shook his head.

'Aw shit,' said Billy Dunston.

'What about the money?' Alex asked.

Murray shook his head again. There was cursing and angry shouts from the group, but Alex just gazed at them in his cool, unruffled way.

'Murray . . . Roy,' he said when the others had quietened. 'Thanks to you two, I'm working on a low-budget level. Now I tried to have some leaflets printed up cheaply. Waycross, come up here and tell me what you think of this.'

Alex held up a leaflet. Murray walked through the seats and up to the podium where he took the leaflet from Alex. He stood there, scowling at the writing, moving his lips, mumbling, 'Chicanos taking our jobs . . . the blacks . . . conspiracy of the Jews . . .' Finally he looked up at Alex. 'Why, this is terrible, Alex, just terrible.'

'Tell everybody why,' Alex said, gesturing to the audience.

Like a kid in *Show & Tell*, Murray held up the leaflet to show everyone. 'Well, as you can see, the printing is for shit. Your "Chicanos" is all blurry here, and your "Jews" is runnin' off into the margin.'

The small crowd laughed appreciatively. Seeing that, Murray started to laugh. The laughter grew. Even Alex started to chuckle. Roy, however, looked on in silence. He was beginning to feel a bit queasy.

'Funny, isn't it?' Alex said. 'Imagine trying to recruit new members with amateurish junk like this.'

'No fuckin' way,' Murray shook his head. He was laughing so hard he had to wipe the tears from his eyes.

Suddenly Alex no longer thought it was funny. He stared at Murray. That cold hypnotic stare.

'You're going to Silhouette City, man,' he muttered.

Murray stopped laughing.

They walked over to the big building in a group. Much to Roy's astonishment, Murray didn't look frightened at all. Instead he popped a couple of sticks of Juicy Fruit gum into his mouth and started chewing like a baseball player. Inside the target range Alex told him to go stand in front of the cop silhouette. Murray marched into Silhouette City like he was going to accept a diploma or something. He turned and faced the group and crossed his arms. He even smiled a little. As Alex picked up the MAC-10 and threw the bolt, Roy shuddered, waiting for Murray's expression to melt into terror. Come on, those were real bullets and Alex's aim wasn't all *that* good. But Murray just stood there with his arms crossed, an almost smug expression on his face.

RaT-tAT-tAT-tAT-tAT . . . the automatic weapons fire roared through the room. Roy and the others had to cover their ears with their hands as flames and smoke burst from the barrel of the gun. Remarkably, Murray stood tall, arms crossed, chewing gum, almost smiling through the entire barrage. Finally, Alex stopped firing and turned to his men who were staring at Murray in awe.

'This man,' Alex said, 'is a warrior. Does anyone doubt that?'

Everyone shook their heads.

'Good,' Alex said, a small angry smile creeping across his lips. 'Now I feel some unity in this room. Now I feel some power. Not a bunch of small-time car thieves and penny-ante codeine junkies and wife-beaters and drifters without a clue in the world, but warriors, united to seize everything that's been denied them.'

Roy watched how the group hung on every word. Warriors. Boy that sounded good. Only Roy didn't feel much like a warrior. He felt more like a small-time car thief, drifting codeine junkie, wife-beater.

'Waycross and Roy,' Alex said. 'You go back to that sister's house. Stay out of sight and wait. In five days I guarantee you will have all our money back and we will deal with the female.'

The early morning sun streamed through the window and woke her. Lou Ann opened her eyes. The redness of the room startled her. Red walls, red bedding, red furniture. This was definitely a room that was meant to be darkened most of the time. The skip tracer snorted and flinched. She'd noticed that he was a troubled sleeper, moving and mumbling all night. It could've been bad dreams, or perhaps just the discomfort of sleeping in a chair. Anyway, Lou Ann was in no rush to wake him. She luxuriated in the large soft bed for a few moments, reflecting. What a strange couple of days it had been. One morning she woke up in the front seat of a car, the next morning in a huge round bed in a casino hotel. If only it was real, and not just some wild dream financed with counterfeit cash.

Tommy woke up while she was speaking to room service: 'Yes, the biggest glass of orange juice you have. Buttermilk pancakes, Canadian bacon . . . OK, fresh fruit, coffee' – she glanced over and saw that he was up – 'make that two coffees, and two eggs sunnyside, hash browns and sausage. OK, thanks.' She hung up.

'Enjoying the good life, huh?' he said, stretching.

'Why not?' She got up and walked past him. 'It may be a while before I have another chance.'

'Hey, where're you going?' he asked.

'To take a shower. You could probably use one too,' she sniffed.

'And I bet you'd just sit here and be a good little girl while I took one,' he said.

'Well, we could take one together,' Lou Ann teased. 'That way you could keep an eye on me.'

'Very funny.'

'Seriously, though,' Lou Ann said. 'I am going to have to ride all the way back with you.'

'Listen, pal,' Tommy said. 'That's just too bad. And besides, compared to where you're going, I smell like a rose.'

Lou Ann went into the bathroom and took a long hot shower. She didn't want to be reminded of where she was going. God, it was so unfair. Even the police knew she was innocent and just covering up. There should've been some kind of exception in the law for people who couldn't turn state's evidence for fear of being murdered.

She got out of the shower and pulled on a big fluffy white bathrobe supplied by the casino. Outside she heard the doorbell ring. The skip tracer answered it. She came out and found him signing the bill.

'Wait,' she said, going to the sack of money. She pulled a $50 bill out and handed it to the room-service boy, who accepted it with wide eyes.

'Gee, thanks, really, thanks a lot,' he gushed, staring incredulously at the denomination.

'No sweat,' she said and winked.

The boy left and she and the skip tracer sat down at the table to eat. She noticed a slight smirk on his lips.

'Oh, come on,' she said. 'This is the only time in my whole life that I get to feel like a big tipper.'

Lou Ann took a long sip on her glass of orange juice. Tommy dug hungrily into his eggs and hash browns. Something was starting to bother him.

'Hey, let me look at that playdough, would you?' he said.

Lou Ann stuck her hand in the bag and pulled out a handful of bills like they were potato chips. Tommy picked a couple up, held them to the sunlight and studied them closely. Fifty per cent of all the counterfeit bills came from abroad these days. A lot of it from Italy, where they bleached down $1s to the bare cotton and linen slips and then reprinted them as $50s and $100s. Tommy squinted at the edges of the bills. This stuff hadn't been bleached.

'You know, it's funny,' Lou Ann said. 'But I haven't had a bit of trouble spending these bills.'

'And I don't suppose you will,' Tommy said, putting the bills down and sipping his coffee. 'They're real.'

Lou Ann stared at him. Then laughed. 'No, no, they can't be.' But his expression said they were. 'How do you know?'

'Believe me, they're real, Lou Ann,' Tommy said. 'The way these deals work, I figure the Birthright got their hands on some high-quality counterfeit stuff, and then they started to exchange it, bit by bit, for the real thing. Like buying a newspaper with a counterfeit fifty and ending up with two real twenties and change. That fake cash in your trailer was probably the last of it . . .' he dug his hand into the sack and pulled out a bunch of bills. 'Because this is grade A United States government green.'

'You mean, I ran off with a quarter of a million in real money? Birthright money?' Lou Ann gasped, feeling her appetite suddenly diminish. She twisted a napkin nervously around her fingers. 'What's gonna happen to me? What's gonna happen to my son?'

Tommy could see the fear in her eyes. Jesus, why'd he ever accept this job? Goddamn Buddy . . . *he* knew what was going down here. It was a no-win situation. He brought her in, those Birthright scum would kill her son. He let her go, the Birthright would kill *her and her son*. Well, damn it, it wasn't his problem. He couldn't be responsible for everyone's personal problems.

'Look,' he said, getting up. 'I have a job to do. We'd better hit the road.'

She started working on him the moment they got in the Fury. Why couldn't he give her just a few more days? Just so she could see the kid, maybe arrange for Jasper to go some place where he'd really be safe. Someplace like Alaska. She'd met a man once who'd said there were little out-of-the-way towns up there where people didn't care if you were on the run and hiding out. OK, so maybe she'd been wrong for getting involved with Roy and allowing the Birthright to leave the counterfeit money in the trailer. Maybe somehow she deserved to be punished for simply trying to be a good wife and mother. But how could this skip tracer allow an innocent child to suffer? Was that right? Was that fair?

'Listen,' Tommy started to say for the hundredth time. 'What's right and what's fair really isn't my—'

BOOM! It sounded like a shot and Tommy thought they were shooting at him. How the hell? He quickly looked around and saw that they were the only car on this thin, dusty strip of highway in the middle of the desert, nothing but sagebrush and tumbleweed for miles.

The car started pulling hard to the right. Aw hell, it was a flat. He pulled off on to the shoulder and gave Lou Ann a look. Then he got out, slamming the door behind her, and took the jack and spare out of the trunk.

'God caused this flat 'cause he doesn't want you to take me back,' Lou Ann said as Tommy worked the lug nuts off the wheel.

'Oh, God's into blowing out tyres, huh?' Tommy said, wiping the sweat off his brow . The sun was coming up hard and fast and the last place he wanted to be was stuck in this desert. He pulled the old tyre off and threw the new one on and spun the nuts. Lou Ann stood beside him in the sun.

'Please,' she begged. 'I'm just asking for two more days. Just so I can go back to my sister's house and see my baby and . . .'

'No!' Tommy finished tightening the lug nuts, picked up the jack and old tyre and threw them into the trunk. Then he turned and faced her.

'Don't you see that I've already gone clinically insane?' he asked angrily. 'Picking up the money, interfering with your case. I meet you and all of a sudden I'm breaking the law!'

'The law, the law,' she shouted. 'What the hell is the law anyway? I used to sit around in a trailer and read the newspaper, and you know what I read? The same people who make the law break it every day!'

'It's not their law I worry about,' Tommy said, slamming the trunk shut. 'It's my law.'

Lou Ann looked him hard in the eyes. 'Fair enough,' she said. 'Then obey your own law.'

He watched her get in the car and slam the door. Jesus, he thought, what a fucking mess. It was times like this when he wished he'd stayed in the Army.

Something wasn't right, Buddy Donovan thought. Somewhere up around Reno something fishy was going on. He could feel it. He knew Tommy Nowak too well. The man was a fucking pro. He could find a single rabbit turd in a whole barnyard if he put his mind to it. He should've done Lou Ann McGuinn by now. Hell, he should've done her and *two more* skips by now. Instead he was out there somewhere running up the fucking mileage.

The phone rang. Buddy grabbed it. 'Yeah?'

'It's Tom,' the voice on the other side of the line said.

Buddy sat up straight. 'Well, speak of the Devil. Would you mind telling me just where the hell you are and what the fuck you're up to?'

'Trail went cold, Buddy,' Tommy said.

'The trail went cold,' Buddy repeated sceptically. 'What do you mean, the trail went cold? Since when does the trail go cold? You find the trail, you follow it till you track her down. No, I don't like this. You're too good, Tom. I'm having serious trouble with this.'

'Yeah, well fuck you,' Tommy said. 'I'm having trouble with it too. Talk to you later.'

He was going to hang up. Buddy couldn't help thinking of all the mileage he was going to have to pay for. He glanced at a file folder on his desk.

'Wait, Tom!' he shouted into the phone. 'Don't hang up!'

'Why not?' Tommy asked.

'Listen, listen,' Buddy said, leafing through the folder. 'Since you've driven all the way out to Reno you might as well do Albert Bass. We just got a tip he's been seen hanging around the casinos up there.'

In the phone booth Tommy sighed. Another skip was all he needed right now. He couldn't deal with the one he had. But looking for Albert Bass would at least give him time to try and figure out what to do about Lou Ann McGuinn.

'Okay, Buddy, give me the particulars,' he said.

Buddy filled him in, and Tommy reluctantly agreed to take on the job.

'Fine,' Buddy said. 'And then, Tom, uh, you know what "cherchez la femme" means?'

'No, Buddy, why don't you tell me?'

'It's French for *dig up the fuckin' broad!*'

Tommy hung up. He was standing in an ancient telephone booth in an old gas station along the highway. Behind it was a convenience store with a casino and post office inside, and the parking lot also served as a bus stop. It was one of those self-contained places dating back to the days when transportation was a lot slower than it was now. In fact, Tommy wouldn't have been surprised if it had been a stage-coach stop before it became a gas station. Place looked nine days older than God. These days busted gamblers low on gas pulled in and gambled their last dollars in the casino, which was all of ten slot machines and one blackjack dealer. If they won they got enough gas for the rest of the trip home. If they lost they could wire someone for money, or sell the car and buy a bus ticket. Lou Ann was standing by the Fury, sipping a Mountain Dew and watching him expectantly. God, the looks she gave him with those big, bright eyes. Like a puppy in the pound who didn't know it was about to be put to sleep.

Tommy let himself out of the booth and squinted in the sunlight. 'Great. Now I've got a new case. A very mean dude. What am I supposed to do with you?'

'Take me along,' Lou Ann said eagerly. 'Maybe I can help.'

Tommy started to laugh. Of all the dumb, hair-brained . . . Suddenly he stopped laughing. Well, maybe. Just maybe . . .

Murray parked the pick-up across the street from Dinah's house. The house was still empty. Roy pushed open the passenger door and started to get out.

'Where're you going?' Murray asked.

'I dunno,' Roy shrugged. 'Thought I'd take a walk.'

'Stay in the pick-up,' Murray said.

'You serious?' Roy asked. 'You heard what Alex said. It could be four or five days till they come back.'

'Yeah,' Murray replied. 'I heard what Alex said. He said stay in the pick-up and watch the house.'

'Sure,' Roy said. 'But he didn't mean it like . . . literally. I mean, I gotta stretch my legs.'

'Stay in the goddamn pick-up,' Murray ordered ominously.

'You're fuckin' crazy, you know that?' Roy said.

Murray reached for the carbine in the gun rack and the next thing Roy knew, he was looking down the barrel. 'Yeah,' Murray said. 'I'm fuckin' crazy.'

Roy got back in the pick-up.

Lou Ann wasn't quite certain why he wanted her to get back into the red evening gown, but she wasn't about to argue. One thing was for sure, he didn't want her all dressed up just to go back to jail. She stood in the doorway of the gas station casino waiting for Tommy to come out of the men's room. An old man played the slot machines while two middle-aged women sat at the blackjack table with glazed looks in their eyes as the dealer shuffled the cards.

'Bet you can't tell me the most urban states in the United States,' the dealer said.

One of the women glanced at him. 'What do you mean, urban?'

'I mean they got the most people living in and around cities compared to those livin' in the country. Percentage-wise,' the dealer said.

'Well, let's see,' the woman said. 'There's Washington DC. I been there once and all it is is a city.'

'Yeah, but it's not a state,' the dealer said.

'How's about Hawaii?' asked the other lady. 'Awful lot of people live in cities there.'

'Okay, Hawaii's one,' said the dealer. 'What're the others?'

The women looked at each other. 'I dunno,' one of them said. 'New York?'

'Alaska and Nevada,' Lou Ann said from the doorway.

'That's right,' the dealer said with a smile. 'After all, how many people in this state don't live around either Vegas, Reno, or Carson City?'

Lou Ann was proud that she'd figured it out all by herself. She glanced back at the men's room. Seemed like the skip tracer had gone in there an awful long time ago. The door to the men's room swung open and a darkly tanned man wearing a gold lamé sports jacket and large sunglasses came out. His hair was slicked back and he sported a pencil moustache. Lou Ann was about to ask if he'd seen Tommy in there. Suddenly the man grinned.

'My, don't you look swell,' he said in an affected voice. He slid off his shades.

'It's you!' Lou Ann gasped.

'Don't you just love it?' Tommy asked, spreading his arms.

'Oh, God,' Lou Ann laughed. 'Don't talk in that voice! It makes me ill! What did you do to yourself?'

'Just changed clothes, sweetheart,' Tommy answered coyly.

'But your skin,' Lou Ann gasped.

'Amazing what you can do with a tube of Man-Tan, isn't it?' Tommy said, reverting to his old voice. 'Now come on, let's go find Albert Bass.'

As they got into the car, Lou Ann said, 'Bet you can't guess what the most urban states in the country are after Hawaii.'

'Christ, Lou Ann, everybody knows it's Alaska and Nevada,' Tommy said as he started the Fury up. Lou Ann slumped down in her seat.

As they drove back toward Reno, Tommy started to tell her his plan. Lou Ann was kind of surprised at how complex it was. 'How come when you came for me you just walked in and took me by the arm?' she asked. 'No disguises, no plans, no nothing.'

'I didn't expect you to put up much resistance,' Tommy said with a grin. 'Little did I know.'

By the time they got to the strip of bars, adult book stores, bingo parlours and tattoo joints, Tommy had finished laying out the plan, part of which required Lou Ann to drive the Fury.

'You sure you got it?' he asked as he got out and Lou Ann slid into the driver's seat. He went around and got back in on the passenger side.

'Sure,' Lou Ann said. 'There's just one problem.'

'What's that?' Tommy asked.

'Your hair's gotten fluffy.'

Tommy looked in the rear-view mirror. She was right. He took a small tube of styling jell out of the glove compartment. As Lou Ann drove she watched him slick down his hair again.

'I don't believe what I'm seeing,' she said.

'Too much raw dude for ya?' Tommy asked, going back into

his affected voice. 'I can dig it, babe. You know, if my life was a movie, it would carry a warning: "Caution: some scenes may be too intense for younger viewers".'

Lou Ann rolled her eyes. 'OK, OK. Let's say your act works. Let's say you actually catch this Bass character.'

'You mean, *we* catch this Bass character, doll face,' Tommy replied.

'What'd he do anyhow?' Lou Ann asked.

'Oh, nothin' much,' Tommy said. 'Just stabbed a blackjack dealer to death in a Vegas casino. Imagined he was being cheated somehow and went crazy with a ten-inch blade.'

'And where are we going to try and catch him?'

'He's been spotted at Harrah's the last couple of nights,' Tommy said.

Lou Ann concentrated on driving. For some reason it hadn't quite been real to her until he said that. But Harrah's was a real place and she could imagine herself there. And that meant Albert Bass was probably a real person and a real killer, and when it came right down to it she must've been out of her mind to think that trying to capture him would be anything that remotely resembled fun.

'Uh, just out of my natural curiosity,' she said. 'How come you can capture someone in Nevada? I mean, aren't you only authorized for California?'

'Nope,' Tommy said. 'As a guarantor of the court I can work in any state in the union. And, unlike a cop, I can break down any door and smash any lock without a legal warrant. I sort of consider it a full-contact sport.'

'And what exactly will you do when you catch Albert Bass?' Lou Ann asked.

'Turn him over to the local cops,' Tommy said, putting away the tube of jell. 'And I'll do it without getting to know all about him.'

A few moments later he told her to pull over next to Harold's Club Casino. A barker in a striped suit and top hat stood outside the casino with a small megaphone trying to coax passersby inside.

'This looks like a good place,' Tommy said. 'And appropriate, too. They've got one of the finest collections of guns in the world in there, including Jesse James's Colt .44 and Wild Bill Hickok's .32 Smith and Wesson.'

'How come you don't carry a gun?' Lou Ann asked.

'Who said I didn't?' Tommy asked.

'Well, I haven't seen any bulges under your T-shirt,' Lou Ann said.

Tommy grinned. 'Honey, if you're lookin' for bulges, my T-shirt ain't the right place.'

'Ha, ha,' Lou Ann replied.

'Now, remember, wait for my signal,' Tommy said. 'And give me your line one last time.'

'Hello, Albert,' Lou Ann said breathlessly, like Marilyn Monroe. 'I'm Miss Reno Casino.'

'Oh, I just love it,' Tommy said in his affected voice and got out of the car. From his box of tricks in the trunk he took out a cheap gold bag filled with hundreds of fake casino chips.

It didn't take Lou Ann long to realize that he'd left the keys in the ignition. Outside on the sidewalk Tommy turned and winked at her. He knew he'd done it. He was testing her.

Tommy crossed the sidewalk towards the entrance of the casino. I must be out of mind, he thought. Leaving the girl in the car with the keys, walking around in this stupid gold jacket with Man-Tan smeared all over my face. Nothing like trying to make things hard on yourself, Tommy, you old buckeroo.

'Pretty hot suit you got there, son,' the barker said, pointing a bamboo cane at him. 'Why doncha come on in and try your luck. Maybe you'll win enough to afford another one.'

Tommy slid over to the barker and pulled a card and a $50 bill out of his wallet. In a low voice he said, 'Detective John Pecker with a Sacramento PD here to pick up a suspect wanted for mutilating carnival barkers.'

'Really?' the barker's jaw dropped.

'Absolutely,' Tommy said. 'We're pretty sure the guy's here in town and from what we know of the way his mind works, sooner of later he's going to pay you a visit. *Comprende?*'

'Well, what're you going to do?' the barker asked, trembling.

'It's not what I'm going to do,' Tommy said, handing him the $50 bill. 'It's what *we're* going to do.'

It was a great plan, Lou Ann thought with a yawn as she sat in the Fury. There was just one big problem. No one had bothered to tell Albert Bass about it. She'd been sitting there for almost an hour, waiting, torn between running away with the car, and staying to help out Mr Skip Tracer.

'Uh hum.' Someone cleared his throat on the driver's side of the window, startling her. Lou Ann sat up and found herself staring at the naked body of a derelict who was holding open a shabby coat, exposing himself.

'So what do you think?' he asked.

'What do I think?' Lou Ann echoed in shock.

'Yeah.' The derelict undulated his hips just in case she wasn't focusing on the right thing. Lou Ann stared for a moment and thought.

'You know what I think?' she finally said.

'What?' asked the derelict.

'I think it looks like a penis, only smaller.'

It took a while, but finally Tommy spotted Albert Bass lumbering down the sidewalk. There was no mistaking him. Buddy said he'd be about six foot six, with a black beard and a long ugly scar on his right cheek. Tommy nudged the barker and motioned to Lou Ann, who was supposed to get out of the car to play Miss Reno Casino, but instead she was talking to some derelict.

Damn it! Tommy cursed to himself. He had to get her attention, but he couldn't risk letting Bass see him do it.

'Uh, here he is, Mr Hassleback,' the barker announced nervously. 'Our one millionth customer!'

Tommy sprang out in front of Bass and shook his hand. 'This is he?' he shouted excitedly. 'This fine figure of a man is Mister Lucky One Millionth?'

Already a crowd was starting to form around them. Tommy took Bass by the arm and tried to steer him aside. Where the hell was Lou Ann?

'Uh, please forgive the absence of a brass band, Mr Uh . . .'

'Bass. Albert Bass.'

Tommy heard a car start. The Fury? Oh Shit! But there was nothing he could do now expect continue with the scam. 'Uh, sorry, Mr Bass, that I've got no brass, if you'll pardon the pun. But if I may toot my own horn here, I do have some swell gifts for you.'

Bass's eyes widened. Tommy glanced at the Fury and then kept talking.

'Uh, Al, may I call you that? My name is Daryl Hassleback and I'm the senior VP for national promotion for the world famous Harold's Club Casino. Are you familiar with our little operation, Al?'

'Uh, yeah, sure. Like with Vic Damone and, uh, Alan King,' Bass said.

Tommy laughed. 'Like with Vic Damone! . . . That's a classic bit, Al. But yes! Precisely. Like with Vic! And like with one hundred and forty-two gaming tables, four showrooms, deluxe hotel and like with this amazing gift for you!'

'What?' Bass asked eagerly.

Tommy heard a car pull away from the curb. He knew it was the Fury. Aw, shit, he was in trouble now. Not just because Lou Ann was taking off, but where was he gonna put Bass?

'Well, uh . . . an all expenses paid weekend at Harrah's,' Tommy announced. 'On me, Al. Plus are you ready for this? Five thousand dollars in free gambling chips!'

The crowd gasped. Albert Bass shoved his hand into the gold bag to feel the chips. Tommy reached into his back pocket for his handcuffs, but the crowd was pressing in. He needed room.

'Uh, folks,' he shouted, 'if you could just give us a tad more elbow room.'

Trying to be helpful, the barker added his own five cents' worth: 'Yeah, move it, will you? The detective is trying to make an arr—'

Bass straightened up and stared at Tommy with his mouth agape. Tommy tried to get the handcuffs out but it was too late. Bass grabbed the barker and threw him against the skip tracer, sending them both flying. The bag of phoney chips spilled to the ground and the crowd dove after them.

Tommy was at the bottom of a crowd of people. Lou Ann was gone, Bass was gone. He fought his way up and out to the sidewalk. Bass was half a block away, running hard. Tommy could tell by the way he was flying down the street that there was no chance of catching up with him, but he had to try anyway. If Bass got away and went into hiding, it would take weeks to find him.

Suddenly the Fury shot down the street with Lou Ann at the

wheel. Tommy couldn't figure out what the hell was going on. A moment later the Fury caught up with Bass just as he was reaching the corner. Bass started across the street. Lou Ann made a sharp right.

BANG! Tommy could hear the collision half a block away as Bass ran straight into the side of the car. Bass went down and Lou Ann got out, raising her fist in the sky and waving at Tommy. But she couldn't see Bass on the other side of the car, getting to his knees.

'Watch it!' Tommy shouted as he sprinted toward them. But it was too late. Bass grabbed Lou Ann, threw her out of the way and jumped into the Fury. Tommy felt a fury of his own. The idea of some skip using *his* car to escape simply enraged him. Just as the car was pulling away, Tommy dove, grabbing on to the door frame.

The Fury was accelerating. Tommy was holding on to the door frame with one arm while he tried to hit Bass with the other. Meanwhile Bass tried to steer and trade punches at the same time. They swerved and screeched down the street, on to and off the sidewalk half a dozen times, scattering pedestrians in every direction.

Tommy had the better angle and managed to land half a dozen hard lefts to Bass's face and mouth. Finally he got in a good one to Bass's nose and felt the bone shatter like tried wood. Bass lost control of the car, which swerved hard to the right and jumped the curb. Tommy jumped off and rolled onto the sidewalk.

Crash! The Fury, with Bass in it, smashed into the Flamingo Casino. Glass, wood and brick flew everywhere. Dazed gamblers reeled around, stunned as playing cards fluttered through the air and chips rolled on to the floor at their feet. There was a mad scramble as others tried to gather up the chips. Tommy crawled over the broken tables and chairs to the Fury. It was wrecked. The front end had smashed in like an accordian, and steam hissed out of the perforated radiator. He yanked open the door and pulled Bass out. Blood was dripping from the man's forehead and nose and he appeared to be dazed, but otherwise all right. Tommy slapped the handcuffs on.

'Mr Bass, my name is Tom Nowak,' he gasped. 'I have been empowered by the state of California to deliver you to the local authorities pending extradition to . . . aw, screw it, you'll find out.' He pulled open the rear door and threw Bass into the cage.

A moment later Lou Ann arrived, out of breath, her eyes wide with excitement.

'Wow,' she gasped. 'Just like you said. It's a full-contact sport!'

Tommy glared at her. 'It wouldn't have to be . . . if someone had kept up their part of the deal.'

Half an hour later the Reno PD took Bass away and a big red tow truck from Cantor's Wrecking Service took the Fury. The car was totalled. Tommy felt like he'd lost his best friend.

'Hey, come on,' Lou Ann said, trying to cheer him up out on the sidewalk as workers began to board up the casino with sheets of plywood. 'It was only a car.'

Tommy glared at her. Only a car? What the hell did she understand about the mystical bond between a man and his machine?

'So what happened?' he asked. 'You were supposed to play Miss Reno Casino and give him a big kiss.'

'Oh, come on,' Lou Ann said. 'We both know what I was really supposed to do. I was supposed to show you once and for all if I'd run away or not.'

'And you showed me all right,' Tommy replied. 'You ran.'

'I thought about it, yeah,' Lou Ann admitted. 'I mean, who wouldn't? But when I saw you chasing him, I came back. I mean, we did Albert Bass. We're partners!' She latched on to his arm as they walked, still jittery from all the excitement.

'Partners?' Tommy yanked his arm away. He could hardly believe what he was hearing. 'Listen, I don't have partners. I don't even have a fucking car any more.'

7

There was another car available, however. It weighed nearly two tons, was powered by a 345-horse-power V-8 engine fed by tri-power Eldorado carburation, got twelve miles to the gallon highway and eight in city traffic, featured lots of chrome with a white and black leather interior and a convertible roof. It was pink and it was still parked in the lot at the Bally Grand.

Twenty minutes later Tommy and Lou Ann stood beside it. Lou Ann took out the keys and dangled them in front of Tommy.

'I don't like it,' Tommy said.

'Oh, I don't know,' Lou Ann said. 'It sort of grows on you after a while.'

'I don't mean the car,' Tommy said. 'I mean the idea.'

'Why not?' Lou Ann asked.

'Because it's dangerous,' Tommy said. 'Didn't anyone ever tell you that it's dangerous to mess around with another man's vehicle?'

'Oh, *please* don't start that with me,' Lou Ann said between gritted teeth. 'As a matter of fact, yes, it has been pointed out to me. Do you want the damn "vehicle" or not?'

'Yeah, OK, I guess I want it,' Tommy said, taking the keys. 'but just for two days. One day for you to see your kid, and one day to get you back to Sacramento.'

'Thanks,' Lou Ann said with a smile. 'You won't regret this.'

'I wonder,' Tommy muttered.

The floor of the pick-up truck was a sea of garbage, littered with Styrofoam cups and hamburger wrappers from every take-out place imaginable, plus beer cans and wine bottles. Roy was certain he had bed sores on his ass from sitting so long. He kept wondering how those astronauts could possibly survive in space for weeks on fuckin' Tang and that processed food shit you squeezed out of plastic tubes.

'Man, I'm glad I'm no astronaut,' he muttered, gazing up at the moon.

'Huh?' Murray, zoned out on pills, was forever watching his sideview mirror for Lou Ann's sister's car.

'I said I'm glad I'm no astronaut,' Roy repeated.

'Yeah, me too,' Murray mumbled.

'Look,' Roy said. 'Maybe I'm thick, man, but I think this sucks, waiting and waiting for . . .'

Suddenly Murray sat up in his seat grinning like a maniac. 'You are thick, darlin', you're just about as thick as a Texas steak. Look here.'

Roy turned around and looked over the seat. A set of headlights was coming toward them. It was Lou Ann's sister Dinah and her husband Jeff in a white Chevette. And it looked like they had Jasper with them.

Roy and Murray stayed in the truck while Dinah and Jeff went into the house with the baby. Murray was reaching for the carbine when Roy grabbed his arm.

'Don't forget one thing, man,' Roy said, trying to muster up as much courage as he could. 'That's my kid. I don't want nothing to happen to it.'

'Sure.' Murray hopped out of the truck and started towards the house. Roy took out his .45 and followed.

They knocked on the door and saw Dinah peek through the blinds. As soon as she saw them, the expression on her face turned to terror. They could hear her through the thin wooden door, gasping, 'It's Roy! Oh, God. It's Roy and some other guy!'

Then they heard Jeff say something about a Colt. Murray gave Roy a look and then hauled back and kicked the door in. Dinah was standing in the middle of the room, cowering with the baby. Jeff was near the bedroom, a long-barrelled pistol in his hands, fumbling with some bullets. Murray raised the carbine at him and he let the pistol drop to the floor and stood with his hands up, trembling. Murray grinned.

'Fella here kinda misses his wife,' he said, gesturing to Roy.

'Where is she, Jeff?' Roy asked, hoping no one would notice

that he too was trembling. He pointed the .45 at his brother-in-law. 'You better tell me right now!'

'I swear, Roy,' Jeff stammered. 'We haven't seen her.'

Murray gave Roy a look which said, that's bullshit and you better do something about it fast. Roy stepped towards Jeff, holding the gun on him.

'Come on, now, Jeff,' Roy said, trying to be cool and talk in a low voice the way Alex did. 'You're my brother-in-law.'

Jeff didn't reply. Roy shoved him back against the wall, but there was no anger in his effort. The next thing he knew, Murray strolled casually across the room. *Wham!* Without a word of warning he smashed Jeff in the face with the butt of the carbine. Jeff's eyes rolled up into this head and he went down. Dinah screamed and ran towards her husband.

'You bastard!' she shouted at Murray. 'What'd you have to do that for?'

'Family members should always be truthful with each other,' Murray said, standing over Jeff's motionless body.

'He was telling you the truth,' Dinah sobbed.

The baby started to cry. Suddenly Roy wanted him. 'Gimme the kid,' he shouted. 'Gimme my flesh and blood.'

Dinah reluctantly handed Jasper to him. Roy had some difficulty juggling the kid and the .45, but he managed. Murray came over and tickled Jasper's chin.

'This kid is our ace in the hole,' he said. 'Mothers always come back for their young. It's just a matter of time.' He turned to Dinah. 'Wouldn't you say so, dear?'

'I don't know,' Dinah said tearfully as she propped Jeff's head up in her lap. A large bruise was turning purple on the side of Jeff's head, but he seemed to be coming around. 'Might be a real long time.'

Murray stretched out on the couch and kept the carbine aimed at them. 'Fine,' he said. 'We'll wait.'

Tommy and Lou Ann were approaching the outskirts of Carson City in the Caddy, the highway ahead of them lit by the car's Guide-matic headlight control. Lou Ann held a Big Mac in one hand and a large diet Coke in the other. Beside Tommy on the front seat was a large bag of fries and a quarter pounder with cheese. He had a large chocolate shake between his legs.

'The way you turned into that Vegas creep was amazing,' Lou Ann was saying. 'Why aren't you an actor or something? I mean, why do you chase fugitives for a living?'

A black-tailed jack rabbit skittered across the highway ahead of them and the Caddy's headlights illuminated a bullet-riddled sign announcing that the Carson City limits were five miles away. Tommy held the steering wheel with one hand and ate with the other. He rarely talked about himself with anyone, but something about her made him feel relaxed and open.

'Tell you the truth, Lou Ann,' he said. 'I like driving into strange towns alone. I like the colour of the light in all-night diners. I like to drift through pool halls and bus stations and the places men go when they're on the run. I like the names of the towns out here – Window Rock, Mexican Hat, Winnemucca. And I like the highway at night.'

Lou Ann stared at him, wondering if he'd realized how poetic he'd sounded. 'Hey,' she said, 'which one of us is the fugitive?'

'Yeah,' he said. 'I guess I always have felt like I was on the run.' Then he grinned. Not one of those hard little grins he gave when he was feeling tough, but a wide open expansive grin. A relaxed grin, for once. Lou Ann knew she'd struck a chord.

'Is that why the first marriage broke up?' she asked.

Tommy glanced sideways at her. It had slipped out back up near Reno. Him and his great record of marriages and engagements.

'Well, the first marriage was a joke,' he said. 'We did it during my one foray outside the field of law enforcement. I was bouncing around the minor leagues in the Giants' farm system. I was never home, I saw more cow-towns than a bible salesman.'

'And the second marriage?' Lou Ann asked.

Tommy shook his head. 'A mistake from the word go. I'd just as soon steer clear of that one. The good days are the ones when I can't remember her name. Then I got engaged again about three years ago.'

'Oh, tell me! Tell me!' Lou Ann's bright-blue eyes widened with excitement.

'Well, there's not much to tell,' Tommy said. 'Right after we got engaged she became Miss Aamco Transmission of Fresno.

Honest to God. Now as Miss Aamco she needed a man to stand beside her when she performed her queenly duties, like cutting the ribbon to open a new muffler shop or something. I guess we both realized that I wasn't the guy.'

'So you've never really settled down,' Lou Ann said.

'No,' Tommy said. 'Tell you the truth, I don't think I'm really . . .'

'Wait,' Lou Ann cut him off. 'Let me guess. You're not really the type, right? You're an American wildcat. Can't breed in captivity.'

She started to laugh and he had to admit it was fairly funny. He really didn't mean to portray himself as the tough, lonesome cowboy. It was more of an accident than intentional.

'And for the rest of your life,' Lou Ann said waxing poetic, 'the road will be your only home.'

'I don't know,' Tommy said. 'Someone I trust a lot once told me that the road can get old, too.'

After Murray found out they had one of those electric bug zappers, he insisted they sit out on the back porch. He really loved the snap, crackle and pop every time some winged creature flew into the electric grid. He even seemed to enjoy the acrid, burnt smell. Roy was starting to think Murray was a fan of death no matter what size or shape it came in.

Roy had Jasper on his knee, and was getting him to laugh by bouncing him up and down. Dinah sat nearby, a worried expression on her face as if she thought Roy was going to take a big bite out of the baby. But soon she turned her attention to Murray, who was snorting some crystal off the tip of a hunting knife.

'Isn't it a little dangerous?' she asked. 'Putting that cocaine on a knife?'

'Cocaine is for queers with gold credit cards,' Murray replied gruffly. 'This here's pure methamphetamine, dear, otherwise known as speed. And the *only way* to snort it is off a hunting knife.'

Roy turned back to Jasper, bouncing him some more, making him giggled, feeling his chubby little tummy and legs.

'Cute little fella, isn't he?' Roy said playfully. 'Yeah. He's his da-dums precious precious.'

'Ain't much for rug rats myself,' Murray said. Suddenly he scooped Jasper off Roy's knee and held him up with one hand. Roy watched the hunting knife, which was still in Murray's other hand. Dinah looked on, that familiar horrified expression on her face. Murray bounced the baby a little. 'Every time I look at a rug rat, I just see accidents waiting to happen. But this one's worth his weight in gold. Yeah. This little rug rat's gonna bring his momma back. Idn't dat right, little guy? Bring momma back with all that money.'

Watching Murray with the baby in one hand and the knife in the other just made Roy too damned uncomfortable. With one crazed swipe Murray could sever that child in two. Roy let out a nervous laugh and took Jasper back. Dinah watched him with wide eyes.

'Roy,' she said, 'what are you gonna to do to Lou Ann?'

'We're gonna get the money and the car keys back and just throw the fear of God into her.'

Murray started to laugh. 'The fear of God? What good is the fear of God? She took our hard-earned bread, dear, and she can nail us cold, understand? The fear of God ain't nearly enough.'

After a while Murray got tired of watching the bugs fry and they moved back into the house and put the *Mary Tyler Moore Show* on the TV. Jasper played on the couch. Dinah and Jeff, who sported a big bandage on the left side of his head, looked pretty exhausted, but they were too scared and frightened to rest. Murray sat in front of the TV, playing with the carbine and drinking Jack Daniels. Roy sat near the window with the curtain pulled back slightly, watching.

'See, man, you ought to meet Alex,' Murray told Jeff. 'If you just sat in a room with him for ten minutes you'd understand why you live in this crummy little house. You'd see just how you were cheated out of your birthright, and what you can do about taking back what's yours.'

'This house is fine with me,' Jeff replied, coldly. 'And look, I know what you stand for. My old man fought against it in World War Two.'

Murray sprang to his feet and pointed the carbine at him. 'Maybe I ought to . . .'

'Jesus Christ!' Roy suddenly interrupted. 'It's my car!'

Murray looked up. 'All right,' he told Jeff and Dinah. 'Roy and me are gonna go in the back. When she comes to the door you act like nothin's wrong, understand? If she senses something's wrong and runs, I'm gonna have to cut her down in the street!'

Tommy slowed the Caddy down. There was a Chevette in the driveway and a couple of cars and a pick-up were parked out in the street. Lou Ann started to pile all the baby clothes from Buster's Department Store on to her lap.

'Recognize any of these cars?' Tommy asked.

'Just the Chevette,' Lou Ann said. 'It's Jeff and Dinah's. Thank God they're here!'

Lou Ann was half-way out of the car and Tommy hadn't even parked yet. He pulled over and she hopped out and ran up the front path with her arms full of clothes. Tommy followed, looking carefully around. He noticed a big boot print on the front door.

A plump woman answered the door, smiling awkwardly. She had rings under her eyes and wasn't acting quite right. 'Hi, honey!' she said with the enthusiasm of a deadbeat greeting a bill collector.

Lou Ann hugged her. 'Dinah, this is my friend, Tom Nowak.'

'Hi, Tom!' Dinah practically shouted his name. 'How nice to meet you! Come on in, you two.'

Lou Ann dashed into the house, but Tommy followed reluctantly. All sorts of bells and alarms were going off in his head. Something was definitely not right. In the living room Lou Ann's brother-in-law Jeff was sitting on the couch watching TV with Jasper on his lap. He had a big bandage on the left side of his head. He got up stiffly and seemed to recite his greeting like a novice actor reading from a bad play.

'Hi, sis!' he said. 'Hello, Tom. Uh, welcome. Hey, Jasper, look who's here! Show momma how you can crawl.'

Tears started to roll down Lou Ann's cheeks and she bit her lip as she threw the baby clothes on the couch and beckoned her son to crawl towards her. 'Come here, sweetheart! Come on!'

Tommy watched her for a moment, then glanced at Dinah and Jeff. They both looked like they were about ready to jump out of their skins. Something really crazy is going on here, Tommy thought.

It didn't take him long to find out what the problem was.

Wham! The back door flew open and Murray and Roy burst into the room with guns drawn. Tommy froze. Dinah scooped up Jasper and ran to the far corner of the room. Lou Ann rose and stared at the men.

'Roy,' she said with remarkable calmness. 'What's going on?'

So this is the famous Roy, Tommy thought. He sort of looked like an anorexic Elvis imitator. Roy was staring at him too.

'Maybe you better *tell me* what's goin' on,' Roy told Lou Ann. 'Who's the new bodyguard?'

Lou Ann looked at Tommy and back at her husband. 'He was sent to catch me.'

'Yeah, sure,' Roy smirked. 'You look real caught.'

'By the bail bondsman, Roy,' Lou Ann added.

Meanwhile Murray crossed the room and patted Jasper's head.

'Take your filthy hands off that child,' Lou Ann said angrily.

Murray just grinned and kept stroking Jasper's head. 'You know, people say you can't put a value on human life. That is such absolute bullshit. I can put a value on this little rug rat's life—two hundred and fifty thousand in cash. So let's have it.'

'And the keys to the Cadillac, too,' Roy added.

Tommy knew he was in a spot. As soon as he produced those keys, Roy was going to go ape shit. Sure enough, as he pulled the keys from his pocket, Roy suddenly spun around and aimed his gun at him.

'You had the nerve to drive my vehicle?' Roy shouted. 'I oughta blow your fuckin' head off.'

'Transmission's almost shot,' Tommy said, goading him. 'And the brakes pull a little to the—'

'Shut up!' Murray screamed. 'I don't give a shit about that junker. I mean, fuck the transmission.' He stepped closer to Lou Ann and brought the carbine up to her face. 'Where's our money?'

'It's right where you hid it,' Tommy replied calmly.

'Go check it out, Roy,' Murray said, keeping the carbine on Lou Ann. 'If the money's there, honk the horn and wait outside. You hear me? You . . . wait . . . outside.'

They all knew what he meant. He might just as well have announced that he was going to blow Lou Ann's head off.

'Uh, Murray,' Roy said, reluctant to leave.

'*You heard me!*' Murray shouted at him.

Roy slowly opened the front door and went outside. As unobtrusively as possible, Tommy looked around, trying to get the feel of the situation, looking for an opportunity. Meanwhile, Murray swung the carbine on him.

'We got some unfinished business with this bitch,' Murray said, appraising Tommy. 'Now you gonna try to be a hero?'

'Hey, man, I'm just a skip tracer,' Tommy said with a shrug. 'This ain't my fight.'

Murray smiled and poked Lou Ann with the nuzzle of the carbine, pushing her towards the back of the house. Tommy knew he was going to have to gamble and fast. He quickly reached down and yanked out the .22 he kept in a leg holster. He managed to get one shot off, hitting Murray in the side. As the force of the bullet spun Murray around, Lou Ann gave Tommy a look as if to say, *'I knew you had a gun!'*

In a flash, Murray swung around and fired a spray of lead. Bullets ripped through the walls, the TV screen shattered and a picture fell. Dinah screamed, everyone dove to the floor. Tommy ducked behind the couch. As an afterthought, Murray swung the carbine around on Lou Ann. Tommy shot him in the thigh and Murray went down to his knees spraying more shots back.

The front door flew open and Roy dashed in, his .45 in one hand, the car keys in the other. He aimed the .45 at Tommy, but Jeff slapped it out of his hand. The keys to the Cadillac jangled to the floor.

'The kid!' Murray grunted, pulling himself up and limping toward them. 'Get the kid!'

Roy grabbed Jasper. Every time Tommy raised his head to take a shot, Murray let go a blast from the carbine, ripping the top of the couch to pieces.

'Come on, Roy,' Lou Ann shouted. 'You're not like them! Give me the baby!'

Murray spun around and Lou Ann dove into the bedroom, screaming as a hail of bullets ripped through the wall behind her. Murray and Roy got out the front door and ran to the pick-up with the baby. Lou Ann started to run after them, but Tommy tackled her. A split second later a barrage of lead shattered the windows near the doorway as Murray covered their escape. Lou Ann looked at Tommy wide-eyed and breathless.

Both of them knew she would've been hit if Tommy hadn't grabbed her.

Tommy crawled to the window just in time to see Roy push Murray into the passenger seat of the pick-up, then climb into the driver's seat with the baby and tear out of there. He got up and went outside. A thick trail of blood ran down the steps, across the yard and into the street. Way down the road the pick-up turned a corner and disappeared. Tommy doubted he could catch them. He turned around and went back inside. The house was a disaster – shattered, overturned furniture all over the place, the acrid smell of burnt gunpower hanging in the air. Dinah was sobbing in Jeff's arms. Lou Ann came through the smoke, her clothes torn, looking like a zombie. Tommy put his arms around her and she hugged him tightly and started to cry.

The baby was struggling. Roy held him in one arm and drove with the other. Next to him, Murray was slumped down in the seat, a large dark-red stain on his plaid shirt slowly spreading across his chest. Roy's eyes were watery and he had to blink the tears away in order to see. He felt them roll down his cheeks. He wasn't certain why he was crying. Nor was he certain why he was racing away. Or even where he was going. Maybe he should've been headed in the other direction. He might lose his wife and kid, but at least he'd get his car back. Where the hell was he going anyway? Back to the camp? What the hell was he doing?

Next to him, Murray coughed. Blood was running out the side of his mouth and down his chin.

'That dude was slick,' he wheezed. 'I'll give him that. "Not my fight," he said. You know what, darlin'? He *lied*.'

'Yeah, shit.' Roy smirked. 'Wonder where Lou Ann found him, huh?'

Murray didn't answer. The baby had stopped struggling and was cooing.

'Hey, Murray?' Roy said. He glanced over at him. Murray's eyes were wide open in a death stare. Oh, shit, Roy thought. Oh shit, oh shit, oh shit . . .

8

They tried to calm down and get the house cleaned up. Jeff went to get his home insurance policy to see how the insurance company dealt with 'damage caused during a gunfight', and Dinah tried to rustle up something to eat. It was kind of weird, but suddenly they were all famished. Tommy could tell they were sort of giddy and trying not to admit it. Cheerfulness was just the wrong emotion to be feeling at that particular moment, since Roy had taken Jasper and they had no idea what those Birthright maniacs might do to the child. It was strange, but an incident like the gunfight, when human lives were flung around like pillows, almost always left Tommy hungry and light-headed, as if those were the body's natural reactions to close calls. He stayed near Lou Ann, who alternately broke into tears over Jasper or went giddy in the afterrush of having survived the gunfight.

After dinner, eager to get away from the smell of burnt gunpowder, they sat outside on the porch. It was very late, but all of them were too full of adrenalin to even think about sleep. Lou Ann sat on the old porch swing, refolding the baby clothes she'd brought in for Jasper. Tommy sat next to her. Dinah hovered nearby, wearing a cardigan and watching her sister closely.

'It's kind of chilly,' Tommy said.

Lou Ann nodded. Tommy took off his denim jacket and draped it over her shoulders.

'Better?' he asked.

She nodded again and kept folding the clothes. Tommy couldn't tell exactly what she was thinking about. The sparkle had gone from her blue eyes, and Tommy realized she was still in shock at having lost Jasper.

'Listen,' he said. 'We'll find your boy. I swear it.'

It was almost as if Lou Ann hadn't heard him. She glanced over at her sister. 'Dinah,' she said. 'Remember what it was like the night he was born?'

'Well, I . . .' Dinah began to reply, but Lou Ann went on talking as if the question wasn't one she'd really expected an answer to.

'I was lying on the table in the delivery room, worrying so much,' Lou Ann said, gazing off into the dark. 'Worrying about Roy because he was in jail, worrying about money, worrying about this baby 'cause he seemed to have two strikes against him even before he was born. And then all of a sudden I just floated up to the ceiling, and I kind of . . . what's the word? Hovered. Yeah, I hovered there, looking down at myself on the table. And I saw how pale and sweaty and worried I was, and I thought, "Oh, it's too bad she's had to be so scared all her life, doesn't she realize everything will be OK?" Because the real me was floating above it all, and the ceiling of the delivery room opened up so that I could keep rising into the air, and it felt like all the stars were passing right through me, and then the baby came out.'

Tommy and Dinah hung on her words, waiting for her to keep going, but Lou Ann suddenly stopped and blinked as if she'd just snapped out of a trance. Tommy thought he could almost see her mind work, going from the night her baby was born to this night, eight months later with the baby gone and no doubt in mortal danger. Lou Ann buried her face in her hands and started to sob again. Tommy put his arm around her shoulders and hugged her.

'We'll find your son,' he told her. 'I promise you.'

None of them managed more than an hour or two of sleep that night. Early the next morning, Tommy was dressed and eager to leave. He didn't say it, but deep down he knew that every second the Birthright had Jasper the danger increased. As an extra precaution he stuck Roy's .45 in his belt. He'd been dealing with outlaws all his life. The violent ones were impulsive, irrational and paranoid. All Jasper had to do was cry at the wrong moment or spew up in someone's car and one of those goons might stomp him without a second thought. He waited as patiently as he could while Dinah and her sister embraced and bade each other a tearful farewell, then he gently guided Lou Ann to the Cadillac. A few moments later they were on the road.

Lou Ann continued to sniff and sob quietly.

'Come on, Lou Ann,' Tommy said. 'You gotta have a positive attitude.'

'Why?' Lou Ann sniffed.

'Because . . . uh.' Tommy didn't have a decent answer. He simply knew he had to keep her sane. 'Look, you want to be partners? Let's be partners. Open the glove compartment.'

Lou Ann reached forward and tried, but it was locked. She shrugged and gave him a helpless look.

'All right,' Tommy said. 'Here's your first skip-tracing lesson. A subtle, almost diabolically clever way to obtain documents from locked places.'

Tommy leaned over and smacked the glove compartment as hard as he could. It fell open. Through her tears, Lou Ann smiled.

'That *is* clever,' she said.

'OK, now let's see what he's got,' Tommy said. Keeping one eye on the road, he watched as Lou Ann pulled out a cheap-looking booklet entitled *The Coming Bloodbath* by one Alex Guidry, no doubt a stellar member of the Birthright ranks. Next came a two-shot Derringer, followed by a rolled up glossy magazine with two naked people embracing on the cover and the catchy title, *Hot Lust*. Next came some keys and a California driver's licence showing Roy's face but issued to a 'William Hollyfield'. Lou Ann noticed that Tommy took extra interest in this last item.

'It's probably not that important,' she said. 'He always had a couple of phoney IDs around. Does look pretty good though, doesn't it?'

'Good?' Tommy took the licence and scrutinized it closely as he drove. 'It's a lot more than good. This thing would fool any trooper in California. This is a Ricky Z original.'

The next thing Lou Ann knew, Tommy hit the brakes and did a fast U-turn. 'Looks like we're heading east,' he said.

'Wait a second,' Lou Ann said, bewildered. 'Who is Ricky Z?'

It wasn't everyday Roy got to drive around in a pickup with a dead man and a baby. Originally his idea had been to get back to the Birthright camp as fast as possible, but a new problem had cropped up. After driving down the dusty roads for a few hours, Roy suddenly seemed to realize that this baby was not going to take care of himself. Little Jasper looked up at him, gurgling as a smile crossed his chubby face.

'Oh, shit,' Roy mumbled to himself. 'Oh, shit.'

He needed diapers. And what about something for the kid to eat? That formula shit Lou Ann was always spending money on. A small convenience store was coming up on his right and Roy pulled off the road, parking as far away from the store and other cars as possible. After all, he had a dead man in the pick-up. Roy got out, taking Jasper in his arms, and went into the store.

Before long he'd found diapers, baby wipes, formula, bottles and nipples and brought them up to the cashier.

'That'll be eighteen dollars and sixty-two cents, sir,' the cashier said.

Roy took out his wallet and counted his money. He was six dollars short. Damn it, now what was he gonna do? All of a sudden he had an idea. 'Uh, could you wait a moment,' he said. 'I'll be right back.'

He went back out to the truck. Murray was slumped against the passenger door. Still holding Jasper in one arm, Roy struggled to get the door open and keep Murray from falling out while he took the dead man's wallet. Then he started back toward the store mumbling to himself. 'Damn you, Roy. I guess you can add stealing from the dead to the list of crimes you have perpetrated.'

Back in the store he paid for everything. There was a picnic table under a big fir tree outside and he laid Jasper on it and clumsily changed him, then headed back to the pick-up. He got in and glanced again at Murray, who had started to turn gray. The sight of the dead man made him wonder again. Why was he bringing Jasper back to Alex to be held for ransom? Why was he kidnapping his own son?

'Because you're too scared not to,' a voice in his head replied.

They were up in the high desert now. Nothing but scorched patches of creosote brush, desert mistletoe, smoke tree and tumbleweeds in every direction. Boulders of every size lay scattered about. An occasional Joshua tree stretched its gnarled branches to the sky, and they passed a few golden-yellow blankets of flowers called goldfields. In the distance were mountains.

Nevada had something like 180 different mountain ranges so it was hard to say just which one this was.

Tommy was always a little wary about driving through these long stretches of nothingness. Almost ninety per cent of the state was owned by the government, and God only knew what weird experiments they were doing out here with chemical and nuclear weapons. It was a well-known fact that some years back a Basque sheep herder up near Winnemuck came out one morning and found that half his flock had mysteriously died over night. He had found them lying around on their backs, stiff legs in the air like some weird cartoon. Of course it was all supposed to be hushed up, but word of these things always slipped out.

Up ahead he saw a rusty-looking sheet-metal warehouse near the side of the road.

'I hope that's it,' Lou Ann said.

'It is,' Tommy answered, turning in past the peeling psychedelically painted sign that said, 'NIRVANA PUBLICATIONS'. The car kicked up a cloud of dust as it stopped, and Tommy got out and pushed a buzzer.

A few moments later the door opened and a bearded man with a ponytail came out. He was wearing a multi-coloured tie-dyed T-shirt and worn-out jeans.

'Hey, Tommy Nowak!' he said. 'How's the life force treating you this afternoon?'

'Not bad, Ricky.' Tommy shook his hand. 'How's about you?'

'Everything's in alignment far as I know,' Ricky said, with a smile that revealed a number of rotten or missing teeth. He glanced at Lou Ann and back at Tommy. 'Just stop by to say hello or is there somethin' I can do you for?'

'I think there's something,' Tommy said, waving Lou Ann to join them.

Stepping into the hot, dusty warehouse, Lou Ann knew she wasn't going to be thrilled with this. She hated dark, dusty places and this couldn't have been worse. The front of the warehouse was filled with stacks of old publications. In one corner was an old printing press that looked like it hadn't been used in ages. In the other corner was an old Volkswagon bus up on cinderblocks, painted psychedelic colours.

Ricky led them into a room in the back where he spent most of his time. Here an old air conditioner grumbled in the heat. There were teetering file cabinets, photo machines, printing presses and cutting boards. Stacks of blank documents, social security cards, driver's licences and phoney credit cards sat on practically every flat surface. The Grateful Dead's live version of 'St Stephen' was playing on a sophisticated CD player, and a yellow joint was smouldering in a tin ashtray. Lou Ann couldn't help but shudder at the sight of it all. Ricky was one strange guy.

Ricky closed the door tightly behind them to keep the cool air inside. 'OK, dude, what's up?'

'What do you remember about William Hollyfield,' Tommy asked, handing him Roy's licence.

Ricky stared at it for a moment and then closed his eyes. 'Oh, dig it, I remember. Went into a trance to come up with that name.'

Tommy looked at Lou Ann and chuckled. Lou Ann scowled back at him.

'You laugh, man,' Ricky said. 'But it's true. The dude was so shaky, and his partners were all so hostile. Speed freaks, man. So I wanted a name that would cool him out, and like I meditated on it, and like it just came to me, like I started to hear it. William Hollyfield, William Hollyfield . . .'

Another lunatic, Lou Ann thought. She glanced at Tommy. Somehow, I get involved with this man and all I meet are lunatics. Then again, she had to admit that she'd met a fair number of them before Tommy too. She noticed Ricky Z was giving her the eye.

'Hey, you haven't introduced me to your old lady yet,' he said.

Tommy flinched at the words 'old lady', but there wasn't much he could do except laugh it off. 'Hey,' he said. 'You're the master of make-believe names. What do you figure her for?'

'I would make her a Gwendolyn, or a Samantha, maybe,' Ricky said, holding up his hands and framing her face. 'But given the way this world is, man, I guess she's probably a Bonnie Sue.'

'Close.' Lou Ann laughed. 'Very close. It's Lou Ann.'

'Some people see the names that are,' Ricky said mystically. 'I dream the names that should be.'

Tommy could see that Ricky was about to launch into one

of his weird dissertations about the nature of names. Unfortunately Jasper was out in the wilderness somewhere and time was precious.

'Listen, Ricky,' he said impatiently. 'About this guy on the Hollyfield licence, and the guys who came with him.'

But Ricky was already off on another track. Taking Lou Ann gently by the shoulders, he guided her towards a photo machine and had her stand on a red X on the floor.

'Let me create a new identity for you, my dear,' he said, ducking behind the camera.

'Did you recognize his running buddies?' Tommy asked.

'Yeah,' Ricky said as he focused the camera. 'The dudes from the Birthright. They're clients of mine.'

'*Clients?*' Tommy said, not trying to hide his shock. 'Damn, Ricky, they're fucking psychos!'

'Aw, they're just a bunch of fuck-ups,' Ricky said. A strobe started bursting as he snapped photos of Lou Ann. 'They just like to play with guns.'

'Come on, Ricky,' Tommy said. 'You know as well as I do there's nothing more dangerous on the face of the earth than a fuck-up with a loaded .44. And maybe you've forgotten what they did up in Idaho with those plastic explosives. Now try to remember. Concentrate.'

The strobes flashed again. Ricky didn't answer.

'Do you know where their camp is?' Tommy asked.

Ricky stepped out from behind the camera and handed Lou Ann a felt-tip pen and a sheet of paper. 'Please sign the name Gwendolyn de la Croix three times in your most relaxed handwriting.'

Lou Ann started to practise and Ricky turned to Tommy.

'Listen, man,' he said. 'I may be out there, but I'm not an idiot, OK? Don't ask me to rat on the fuckin' Birthright.'

He turned to take the sheet of paper from Lou Ann, but Tommy grabbed him.

'Listen,' Tommy hissed. 'They've got her baby, Rick. An eight-month-old being held by speed freaks with automatic weapons.'

Ricky squirmed. 'What're they doin' with the kid?'

'It's a long story,' Tommy said, 'but the essence of it is we don't have a lot of time. Now how about it?'

'I think their camp is up in the Sierras,' Ricky said with a sigh. 'See, they were all wired the day they were here. I mean, they were talking as fast as auctioneers. And one of 'em kept calling me a hippie, you know? Like trying to fuck with my mind. But I just let him keep on talking, 'cause my mind is unfuckable.'

'Absolutely,' Tommy agreed.

'Anyhow,' Ricky went on, 'he said there was a hippie commune down the road from their camp, over in Mariposa, and come "The Day of the Great Uprising" he was gonna personally carve up every hippie on that farm.'

'All right!' Tommy slapped his hands together.

'What?' Ricky Z asked. 'You think killin' hippies is good?'

'No, no,' Tommy said. 'I'm just glad that you kept your ears open.'

'When you act as weird as me,' Ricky said with a shrug, 'People let down their guard.'

Tommy was itching to go. The thought of little Jasper in the hands of the Birthright was starting to haunt him. Ricky walked them back out to the warehouse entrance.

'So the next time I see you,' Ricky told Lou Ann. 'I'll have Gwendolyn de la Croix all fleshed out.'

Lou Ann thanked him. He may have looked and acted weird, but underneath it all, she'd decided he was just a sweet and slightly lonely guy.

Tommy and Ricky shook hands. 'Now Tommy,' Ricky said, leaning on the Caddy. 'There's a name that fits. Hey, how come you never turned me over to the cops, all these years?'

'People want to disappear and reappear somewhere else, as somebody else,' Tommy said. 'That's America, right? It's all part of the game. They need someone like you around.'

They got back into the Caddy and waved goodbye. Ricky stood by the warehouse and waved back. A hippie forgery expert living alone up in the high desert. To Tommy it somehow seemed very American.

Next to him Lou Ann pulled her hair back to keep it from blowing in the wind. She was happy and eager. 'Next stop, the high Sierras!'

'Do me a favour,' Tommy said, glancing at her as he drove. 'Don't be so eager. The last eager skip tracer I knew wound up dying Szechuan style.'

'Dying Szechuan style?' Lou Ann repeated curiously. 'Is that detective slang?'

'Yeah,' Tommy said. 'It means his face looked like a plate of Chinese food.'

They were doing about eighty, heading back across the desert, the road disappearing quickly beneath the car, but still stretching endlessly before them. Off in the distance a dust devil shimmied and danced like a ghost through the brush. Thinking about what Tommy had just said, Lou Ann took a deep breath.

'OK,' she said. 'I'll try not to be too eager. I guess we'll find them soon enough.'

'Yeah,' Tommy echoed. 'I guess we will.'

They stood on the lush green hill behind the camp. Under the towering pines around the open grave, a dozen armed speed freaks looked down mournfully at the bloodied body of one of their own. Roy held Jasper in his arms a little way from the group, watching the white puffs of clouds in the sky through the cracks in the tree tops. Murray Waycross had lived a violent life and died a violent death. He had, in his own weird way, been consistent. Roy was aware that he did not possess such consistency. Instead he was wracked by doubt and indecision. At moments like this, standing around graves in the solemn forests of the Sierra foothills, Roy could only ask himself, one thing, 'What the fuck am I doing?'

Closer to the grave, the others threw ritual offerings on to the corpse. A pint of wild Turkey, a bone-handled knife, a handful of coloured pills and a single unused cartridge from the carbine. Alex stood at the head of the grave. In his face Roy could see a seething anger, but as always, the man was in control.

'Rest assured,' Alex muttered. 'He will be avenged. It's beyond money now. It's beyond that female. It's a question of paying that lawman back.'

'Amen,' said Billy Dunston, a ragged commando who would

now take Murray's place as the toughest man after Alex, who was, of course, the toughest of them all. Some of the others began to shovel the rocky soil into the grave. Roy had started to take Jasper back down to the camp for his afternoon nap when suddenly he heard Alex call from behind. 'Roy?'

Roy felt himself grow tense. He turned and watched Alex approach and put his arm over his shoulder. Together they started walking toward camp.

'Now, Roy,' Alex said. 'I want you to think. Was there anything in that pink Cadillac that a smart man might have used as a clue to trace us?'

Roy tried to think. It was a question Alex had asked him several times since he'd brought Jasper and Murray back in the pickup. 'No, sir, nothing, I swear.'

Roy felt Alex tighten his grip on his shoulder. '*Think*, Roy.'

'I swear Alex, there was nothing,' Roy whined. 'I'd tell you if—'

'What? What is it?' Alex asked urgently.

'I think,' Roy said, stopping. 'I think I just thought of something.'

They drove up into the pine forests of the Sierra Nevada foothills, passing the scars of old mine shafts, tunnels and diggings still visible from the Gold Rush days. Above them, beyond the timberline, the great granite ribs of the mountains lay naked. Below were the smooth slopes, yellow with dried wild oats and spotted with green oak and fir. It was such beautiful country that it was hard to imagine such ugly things going on in its midst.

Lou Ann soon learned that detective work wasn't a whole lot of fun. It meant plodding slowly, stopping at every possible kind of place Roy might have stopped in and showing Roy's picture on the fake ID to the people behind the counters. She and Tommy tried pharmacists, grocery clerks, liquor-store cashiers, and waitresses, all without luck.

By nightfall they were exhausted. Lou Ann had lost track of the number of towns and out-of-the-way gas stations they'd stopped at. She was beginning to have doubts that they'd ever find Jasper.

'Either we're looking in the completely wrong places,' she said as they rode through the dark in the Cadillac, 'or some of those people had to be lying when they said they didn't recognize him.'

'Now you're starting to see what we're up against,' Tommy said.

'Right now I'd like to be up against a nice soft pillow,' Lou Ann said with a yawn.

A few minutes later Tommy pulled into the empty parking lot of the World O' Wonders Motel. The multi-coloured neon sign flickered in the night sky. Except for the motel office all the rooms looked dark.

'Well,' Tommy asked, 'what do you think?'

'Is there any chance of driving back up to the Bally Grand?' Lou Ann asked.

Tommy shook his head.

'Then this place'll have to do.'

Tommy got out and went into the office. A tall, gawky guy wearing a string tie nervously straightened the calendars behind the check-in desk.

'Modesto is about forty miles north of here,' the clerk began before Tommy could even ask for a room. 'Fresno is about eighty miles south. Just drive due west till you hit Route 99. Make a right for Modesto, a left for Fresno.'

'What are you talking about?' Tommy asked.

'You want directions, don't you?' the clerk said.

'No, I want a room for the night.'

The clerk gaped at him. 'A room? You mean you dont just need directions? You're staying? Fantastic!'

'Is there somewhere I can park the car out of sight?' Tommy asked, pointing through the office window at the Caddy.

'Oh, don't worry, sir,' the clerk said eagerly. 'I can take care of that for you. And I can give you the Hawaiian Luau room!'

'Sounds wonderful,' Tommy said with a sigh.

A few minutes later Tommy led Lou Ann into the room. Lou Ann gasped. Tommy shook his head in wonder. The Hawaiian Luau room was nothing more than a dingy hole with a couple of air-line posters and some photos torn from travel magazines taped to the wall. A dusty plastic pineapple sat on top of a plywood bureau.

'This is unbelievable,' Lou Ann mumbled.

'If there's one thing I'll remember about this experience,' Tommy said with a chuckle. 'It's bound to be the wide and unusual variety of places I slept in.'

111

'It's simply eerie how much this is like Hawaii, isn't it?' Lou Ann asked, walking through the dilapidated room.

'Like we just walked on to the beach at Waikiki,' Tommy said with a yawn. 'Come on. Let's lie down under a palm tree and get a little sleep.'

There seemed to be no question that Lou Ann got the bed again. In his own funny way, Mr Skip Tracer was quite the gentleman. It didn't appear to have occurred to him that he'd be sleeping anywhere but in the chair. A few minutes later he was slumped down, his chin on his chest, arms tucked tightly before him, and his long legs crossed at the ankles. Once again Lou Ann laid in bed in the dark and watched him. This time escape was the last thing on her mind. He might have been able to track men through the most adverse of circumstances, but Lou Ann was beginning to think there was one path he simply had to be led down by hand.

She slid out of the bed and moved towards him, then touched his face lightly.

'Tom,' she whispered.

He stirred.

'Tom?' she said again, stroking his hair.

Tommy opened one eye. An eyebrow arched. Lou Ann took his hand and pulled him up and toward the bed.

'Uh, listen . . .' he began.

Lou Ann quickly put her hand to his lips to silence him.

'We've done enough talking for one night,' she whispered.

She pulled him down. He didn't argue.

Roy wondered if the others ever felt like actors too. Actually, that was the way he always felt. Like he was acting. Like it wasn't real life he was living. At the moment he was riding up into the high desert with Billy Dunston and two of the Birthright's meaner guerrillas, Darrell and Ken-Lee Smith. Roy felt even more uncomfortable than he'd felt with Murray. At least you could talk a little sense into Murray once in a while. These guys were total animals.

'There it is,' he said as the headlights picked up Ricky Z's warehouse. They pulled in front and the men hopped out. Trying to act tough, Roy carried a tyre iron. The other three had guns. They walked up to the door and tried it, but it was locked. Roy tapped the tyre iron against the door and heard the metallic sound echo around inside the warehouse.

'Ricky Z,' He said loudly. 'Yo! Open up, man!'

There was no reply.

'Come on, Rick,' Roy shouted. Secretly, he hoped Ricky wouldn't be there. The guy never went any place, but maybe just this once he was away. Getting no answer, Roy reared back and smashed the door with the tyre iron. He definitely preferred hitting *things* rather than people. The sound resounded through the warehouse.

'Hey, open up!' Billy Dunston shouted. 'Ricky, you stupid fuckin' hippie, we wanna talk to you!'

Roy smashed the door again and again, the hollow echo of the tyre iron ringing loudly in the night. Oh, please, Ricky, he thought, don't be in there. Suddenly the door flew off its hinges. The men crowded through the doorway and abruptly stopped. Ricky Z was standing inside the warehouse, looking terrified.

'Little fuck was standing here all along,' Billy growled.

'I . . . I didn't know who it was,' Ricky stammered.

'Like hell you didn't,' Billy said, giving him a vicious backhand across the face. Ricky hit the ground, but Darrell and Ken-Lee quickly pulled him to his feet and dragged him into the room in the back. They threw him in a chair and stood around him, shouting angrily.

'Was that lawman here?' Billy yelled. 'Did he bring the woman with him?'

'Wha . . . what woman?' Ricky replied, trembling.

Billy answered by grabbing one of the file cabinets and pushing it over into the camera machine with a crash. Official-looking documents and phoney IDs spilled out of the drawers.

'Tell me the goddamn truth,' Billy roared.

'I told you,' Ricky said. 'I've been fasting here alone for three days. I haven't seen a living soul.'

Darrell smacked him in the face, bloodying his nose and lip.

'Don't try to act slick, Rick,' Billy snarled. 'It don't suit you.' He grabbed another file cabinet and toppled it over with a huge crash. Dust and flying papers filled the air. Roy began to wonder if they were wrong. After all, it was just Alex's guess that Lou Ann and the skip tracer would go there.

'Hey,' he said. 'Maybe they really didn't come here, Billy. I mean—'

With Billy's attention momentarily diverted, Ricky leaned towards his work table and tried to slide a manila envelope under some other papers. In a flash, Billy whirled around, grabbed Ricky's wrist and scooped up the envelope. He tore it open and inspected the contents. A smile spread across his lips as he handed them to Roy.

'Didn't come here, huh?' he laughed. 'You ought to check this out.'

Roy took the documents and started at them in disbelief. There was a California driver's licence with Lou Ann's photo and the name Gwendolyn de la Croix. Clipped to it was a birth certificate, an American Express Gold Card and even a goddamn Jack LaLanne club membership. Roy stared angrily at Ricky.

'You lied,' he grumbled, imitating Alex. 'They were here. What did you tell them about us?'

'I told 'em you were somewhere up in the Sierras, near some hippie commune.' Ricky gasped in fear. 'I swear that's all. Honest. I'm too fucking scared to lie, man.'

'When did they leave?' Billy asked.

'This afternoon. Three, maybe four.'

Billy nodded and glanced at Ken-Lee who was strolling nonchalantly behind Ricky. Roy noticed that Ken-Lee had a .44 Magnum in his hand.

'Too scared to lie, huh,' Ken-Lee said softly in *his* Alex imitation. 'Man, I can believe that.' Without warning he smashed Ricky on the back of the head with the gun's butt. Ricky slumped down and slid out of the chair to the floor. For a moment the men stood around, savouring the sight of the unconscious man at their feet.

'Come on, let's trash it,' Billy said. They left the room, slamming the door and locking it behind them. In the warehouse, Billy stopped and looked around.

'Get those rags,' he ordered, pointing at a pile of old rags on the dusty printing press. Near the door he found a large can of printing solvent. He unscrewed the top and took a whiff, then smiled.

Outside Darrell and Ken-Lee stuffed the rags under the warehouse walls. Then Billy splashed the solvent on to them and lit a match.

'This'll teach that scumbag,' he grumbled, lighting the rags.

Roy thought they should've taken off fast, but Billy and the others couldn't resist staying and watching. The fire grew gradually, creeping along the building's foundation. Smoke began to seep out from under the roof. All that paper stacked inside must've been catching slowly, heating the inside of the warehouse like a giant stove. The smoke seeping out of the roof was growing thicker by the moment. Suddenly, something inside exploded, causing the walls to rattle and shake. Darrell let out a whoop and Billy grinned.

The fire was spreading faster now, huge orange and white flames lapping at the walls, causing the sheet metal to twist and buckle. The heat forced the men to move back. Roy's face felt hot like when he was a boy roasting marshmallows around a camp fire. He was certain now that the fire could be seen for miles around. The more intense it grew, the wilder the other men got, shouting and dancing in the firelight like crazed cannibals in the jungle. Roy stood a little off to the side, watching, waiting, knowing that inside a man was being burned alive.

9

The sun rose over the World O' Wonders Motel and its shimmering light pierced the dusty moth-eaten curtains of the Hawaiian Luau Room, disturbing the delicate peace within. Tommy opened his eyes and tried to orient himself. When you were constantly on the move, each morning was a little bit of a surprise. This morning it all came back pretty quickly. He turned and gazed at Lou Ann, asleep with her back towards him. It was the first time in years that he'd woken up in bed with a woman and not only remembered her name, but wasn't hung over and didn't mind being there.

Quietly he slid out of the bed and went into the bathroom. He took a shower, running the water extra hot in the hope that the steam would kill whatever organisms thrived around the drain. After he'd shaved and dressed, he went back into the room, where Lou Ann was still sleeping. A shaft of bright sunlight from the window cut across her shoulders.

'Hey,' he said, gently shaking her. 'We better get going.'

She woke up, saw him, and smiled. Tommy started to rise but she reached up and pulled him down into the shaft of light.

'Wait a second,' she said softly. 'Just one second. I want to look at you in the light.'

Tommy squinted a little and squirmed uncomfortably.

'Don't you want me to look at you?' Lou Ann asked.

Tommy shrugged. The truth was he didn't care for it. The whole idea of someone gazing so openly unnerved him a bit.

'What're you thinking?' she asked.

'Oh, I don't know,' he said.

'Yes, you do.'

'OK, I was thinking . . .' Tommy took a deep breath. He was real bad at this kind of thing. 'I was thinking after we find your kid . . . uh, where are you going to go?'

Lou Ann let her head fall back into the pillow and smiled at him, ever so pleased that he'd asked. 'Oh, I don't know. I guess I'll go some place where . . . you can track me down.'

Tommy smiled back, then straightened up, sliding out of her grasp. It was all very nice, but a little too mushy for his tastes.

Later, when they went to the motel office to check out, the desk clerk was delicately placing a limp bunch of bruised green bananas into a flimsy wicker basket.

'Up already?' He seemed disappointed. 'I was just going to bring you some bananas for your morning luau.'

'Uh, thanks,' Tommy said. 'But we'll have to take a rain check.'

The desk clerk shrugged and started to take the bananas out of the basket. Tommy took out Roy's fake driver's licence.

'By the way, my name is Tom Nowak. I'm a fugitive hunter, State of California, looking for this man. Haven't seen him, have you?'

'Oh, dear,' the clerk gushed. 'That must be an awfully nerve-wracking job! I sure would like to help you out.'

He took the licence and studied it. Of all the people Tommy had shown Roy's picture to in the last few days, he seemed the least likely—

'Oh, yes, I know this man,' the clerk said excitedly.

'He stayed here not more than three or four weeks ago!'

Tommy glanced at Lou Ann. Three or four weeks ago Roy was still living in the trailer with her.

'It's possible,' Lou Ann said. 'I remember him going off on what he said was a fishing trip, only he didn't take a rod. I thought it was kind of peculiar. I suppose he could've come up here.'

'Oh, I am absolutely certain he's the one,' the clerk said. 'And it's funny, but this name is so much better than the one he used then.'

'What was that?' Tommy asked.

'Well, would you believe he signed in as a Mr Dickhead?' the clerk said, thumbing through the guest register and pointing out the signature. 'I mean, really, if I had a name like that I think I'd die.'

Tommy and Lou Ann stared at the signature.

'John A. Dickhead,' Tommy read incredulously.

'That's Roy's handwriting,' Lou Ann said. 'And it's not a bad self-description.'

Tommy couldn't help laughing. 'Wait a minute. A guy registers for one night and calls himself John A. Dickhead and you didn't think maybe it was an alias?'

'Well, you know that was the first thing that crossed my mind,' the clerk said. 'But then I thought, there's a million fake names you could use in this world. Why would you use John A. Dickhead unless you had to?'

'He's got a point there,' Tommy told Lou Ann. Then he turned back to the clerk. 'Do you remember anything else about this, uh, Mr Dickhead?'

'Oh, I'm afraid it's mostly the name I remember,' the clerk said. 'To be honest, I'm not the most observant man in the world. I tend to my own knitting, so-to-speak.'

'Uh, sure,' said Tommy. 'So where's the car?'

'The pink one?' The clerk looked a little uncomfortable.

'Right, the pink one.'

'Well, it's out in the coop.'

'Out in the . . . coop?' Tommy repeated incredulously.

It was worse than he could've imagined. There must've been a thousand pigeons in that coop and from the looks of the Cadillac just about every one of them had used it for target practice. Tommy had never seen anything so disgusting in his life. Next to him, Lou Ann was laughing hysterically.

'Jimminy Cricket,' gushed the clerk. 'Here's one desk clerk who didn't have his thinking cap on straight last night!'

'It's sacriligious,' Tommy said, gazing at the car. 'Thank God the top was up.'

'Oh, does Roy deserve it!' Lou Ann laughed, wiping the tears out of her eyes.

'Well, all I can say, Mr Nowak, is that I'm awfully sorry,' the desk clerk apologized. 'There's a car wash just down the road and I'll be glad to subtract the cost of a wash from your bill.'

Just getting into the car was a trial. Tommy gingerly pulled the door open and slid in. Lou Ann got in next to him. The windshield was pretty bad, but Tommy didn't dare use the windshield wipers. After all, who knew what kind of mess that would cause?

The desk clerk trotted alongside them as Tommy slowly backed the Caddy out of the coop.

'Hey,' he shouted. 'Want to stay in the Wonders-of-the-Orient suite tonight? I've got a wok in there!'

Tommy waved him off and headed down the road towards the car wash. People actually pointed and laughed at the car as Tommy and Lou Ann passed. At the car wash Tommy paid the attendant and then drove the Caddy on to the motorized ramp that would pull it through the washing apparatus. The tyres bounced into the tyre wells. As the machine began to work, Tommy took his hands off the steering wheel and stretched out in the seat. He and Lou Ann watched the liquid soap squirt on the car and then the big rolling brushes sweep towards them over the hood.

'Well, can't say this job doesn't take you to some fairly unusual places,' Tommy quipped.

'Car washes are not unusual to most of us,' Lou Ann replied as the windshield went white with foam. A moment later the brown bristles of the rolling brush cut through the foam, followed by a shower of rinsing water.

Suddenly there were thumps on the hoop and Tommy felt the Caddy's front end dip. As the rinsing water washed off the windshield, two forms appeared on the hood – men holding pistols. Lou Ann screamed. Tommy realized he couldn't go anywhere. The car was stuck on the mechanical track. One of the men was raising his gun. Tommy grabbed Lou Ann and pulled her down under the dashboard.

Crack! A bullet smashed through the patented E-Z-eye windshield and burrowed into the driver's seat, followed by another and another. Tommy was lying on his back under the dashboard. Lou Ann was curled up on the floor below the glove compartment. She gave him a terrified look. Tommy knew they were sitting ducks. There was only one chance. He reached up with his left hand and turned the keys in the ignition while pushing down on the gas with his right. The Caddy started up and roared. Tommy grabbed the shift lever and jammed it into reverse. The car lurched back and the tyres screeched in the tyre wells. They could hear shouts as the gunmen tumbled off the hood. Tommy jammed the car into drive and it lurched forward, the hydramatic transmission whining like a chain saw. Then he threw it into reverse again, creating a rocking motion, as if he were trying to get out of a snowdrift. The car shook and shuddered as it fought against the towing mechanism.

Bullets ripped through the windows and ricocheted off the Caddy's body as it rocked and lurched. Suddenly something snapped and the car shot forward. Still on his back under the dashboard, Tommy could feel the sudden acceleration. They were moving, and fast! Tommy stuck his head up just in time to see that they were flying towards a ditch. He spun the wheel and the Caddy did a 360 on the tarmac.

Another bullet glanced off the bumper as the gunmen jumped into their pick-up. Getting back into the driver's seat, Tommy floored the Caddy past them. Bullets were flying everywhere. Lou Ann tried to look up, but Tommy pushed her head back down.

'Stay low!' he shouted, ducking down himself until he could just barely see the road ahead. A bullet tore through the convertible top. Another shattered the mirror on the passenger side. Tommy kept the Cadillac going flat out, heading west, but the pick-up was gaining. He stayed low and frantically reached into his belt for Roy's .45.

More bullets ripped through the car's top. The pick-up was getting closer. Ahead, a big farm truck loaded with hay lumbered down the highway towards them. Bullets seemed to be flying at them from every direction as the pick-up pulled up beside them. Tommy stuck the .45 out the window and fired. The big farm truck was 100 yards away and closing in. The pick-up was in the eastbound lane, on a collison course with the farm truck as if they were playing a game of 'chicken' with guns. Tommy kept firing. The farm truck was closing in fast, and Tommy knew he had to act quickly, before they all got killed. The pick-up slowed down as if to get back into the westbound lane behind the Caddy, but Tommy slowed too, preventing it from moving over. The farm truck was just twenty-five yards away now. By the time Tommy's attackers realized what was happening, it was too late to stop. Tommy was running the pick-up head on into the farm truck. At the last possible second Tommy pulled hard to the right. The pick-up swerved wildly to the left, went off the road and flipped over.

On the highway Tommy kept the Caddy floored. In the rear-view he could see a couple of the men climb out from under the pick-up and fire their guns, but it was no use. The Caddy was flying.

Lou Ann shakily climbed out from under the dashboard and stared back down the highway at the overturned pick-up. She looked stunned, frightened and relieved. Tommy settled more comfortably in his seat, then reached over and stroked the hair out of her eyes with his finger.

'Hey, listen,' he said with a smile, 'at least we got the pigeon shit off.'

Lou Ann stared at him like he was crazy.

Tommy knew exactly where to go. It was pretty damn obvious and the thing that pissed him off the most was that he hadn't realized it sooner. Putting the car in the pigeon coop was a dead giveaway. How could he be so thick?

He pulled the Caddy into the World O' Wonders parking lot and jumped out. Throwing open the door of the motel office, he marched straight inside. The desk clerk looked startled, but tried to cover it up. Tommy reached across the counter, grabbed him by the string tie and yanked him forwards on the counter. With his free hand he shoved the phone in the clerk's face.

'Holy Toledo!' the desk clerk gasped. 'What's going—'

'Dial it, Mr Dickhead,' Tommy growled, shaking the phone at him.

'Dial what?' the trembling clerk asked. His face was starting to turn red.

'The same number you dialled when you set us up this morning,' Tommy said. 'The number of the Birthright camp.'

The clerk gave him a look like he was crazy. It was a good act, and Tommy showed his appreciation by pulling the string tie tighter. The clerk's face started to turn purple. He started to dial.

Inside the target range, Roy held up a .38, aiming it at the inhabitants of Silhouette City. He was having trouble concentrating. He'd heard about the plan concerning the Caddy and the pigeon coop and it sent a pain deep within him each time he imagined his vehicle covered with bird shit. But he had to admit that it was a good plan, and this caused even more pain. By now Billy and the others must've completed their mission. Lou Ann, no doubt, was dead.

'Wake up, Roy,' Alex hissed into his ear.

Startled, Roy stiffened and squeezed the hair trigger just enough to fire a shot into the target's head.

'Into the kill zone, Roy,' Alex said ominously. 'Solar plexus. Stomach. Always aim into the kill zone, not his damn head 'cause you might miss it. I told you this before. Headhunting is bullshit. Headhunting is high risk. He took your woman, Roy. Blow the fucker away.'

Roy squeezed off another shot, hitting the target in the groin.

'Better,' Alex said.

'Hey, Alex!' Someone shouted from outside. 'Phone call!'

Tommy released the frightened desk clerk. He was sort of looking forward to talking to the leader to this gang of psychos. On the phone he heard bootsteps clunking over a wooden floor and then a low hard voice said, 'Hello?'

'Hello, Alex,' Tommy said. 'This is Tom Nowak. How you doin'?'

There was a moment of silence on the phone. No doubt surprise, Tommy supposed. Then Alex said, 'I'm OK, tracer. I'm doing just fine. Kind of surprised to hear from you though. I thought they'd be scraping you off the upholstery by now.'

'Well, if there's one thing I've learned in life,' Tommy said, 'it's that things don't always turn out the way we think they should.'

'That's very wise, asshole.'

'OK, look,' Tommy said. 'Why don't we cut out all this foolishness and make a straight trade.'

'One male infant for all the money? Even up?' Alex said.

'Right. Talk.'

Alex laid out his plan for the exchange. Tommy listened and scribbled the information down in the margin of a newspaper. Tommy made a few suggestions of his own when he disagreed with Alex's terms, and after a brief but tense talk, they finally came up with a plan they both agreed on.

'Two o'clock sharp,' Alex said.

'Right.' Tommy hung up. The desk clerk was watching him with a regretful, frightened look on his face.

'Listen, Mr Nowak,' he said in a shaky voice. 'I'm really sorry about what happened before. It's just that those men have us so damn scared.'

'It's all right,' Tommy said. He started to go.

'But wait,' the desk clerk said in a low voice, looking around as if he thought the walls had ears. 'There's something that might help. A place over in Coulterville, the Wayfarer Inn. Sometimes they go over there in the evening to have their cocktails.'

Tommy smirked. 'Cocktails, huh? Thanks for the tip.' He went back out to the Caddy. Jesus H. Christ, he thought. *Cocktails?*

10

A light rain was falling, the droplets dripping through the bullet holes in the Cadillac's windshield as Tommy drove to the rendezvous point. Above them low grey storm clouds whisked quickly by. Lou Ann read the directions that Tommy had written on the torn piece of newspaper. They were coming into the most rundown section of a town called Palerump. Half the buildings here had been demolished, leaving big wind-blown spaces filled with garbage and tumbleweed. Most of the other buildings were boarded up. Not a soul was in sight.

'. . . to the corner of Sequoia and DuBrow,' Lou Ann read.

Tommy drove slowly, watching for signs of an ambush. He figured there was a good fifty per cent chance the Birthright would spring one.

'Park near the intersection and leave the keys inside,' Lou Ann read.

Tommy parked the Caddy about fifty feet from the intersection. The rain was starting to come down harder. They got out of the car. Tommy carried a gym bag.

'Leave the money in the dumpster on the northeast corner,' Lou Ann read. 'The baby will be on the southeast.'

They were coming from the north. Ahead to their left was a large green dumpster with 'Matthews Refuse' marked on the side. Tommy and Lou Ann walked cautiously toward it, their legs tight with tension. At the dumpster Tommy looked around once more before throwing the gym bag inside. Lou Ann was already running across the intersection toward the southeast corner.

Tommy jogged after her. On the corner was a vacant lot filled with garbage, debris, worn tyres, old refrigerators, stoves and other appliances. As they neared it, the rain became even heavier, soaking their heads and seeping through their clothes. Through the heavy roar of rain Tommy thought he heard something.

Lou Ann must've heard it too because suddenly she stopped. It sounded like a baby crying. Lou Ann's eyes went wide. It was coming from a pile of old clothes nearby. She ran to it and started digging through the clothes, flinging articles in every direction. Tommy pulled his gun and kept one eye out for an ambush while he helped.

As they dug through the pile, the cries grew louder. There was a lot of old clothing here. Tommy couldn't believe the Birthright would be stupid enough to bury the kid so deeply. Didn't they know it could suffocate? Suddenly the wet air was pierced by Lou Ann's loud gasp. Tommy quickly looked down into the pile and saw that Lou Ann had uncovered 'the baby'. It was a plastic, blue-eyed doll making mechanical baby cries. *Plastic explosives*, Tommy thought. In a flash, he knocked Lou Ann to the side and threw himself on top of her.

The explosion was earth-shattering, showering them with dirt, debris and shreds of clothes. Tommy's head felt like it had been squeezed in a vice and his ears were ringing like church bells. Through the bells he heard the screech of car tyres and looked up just as the Caddy pulled away from the dumpster. Lou Ann was already on her feet, running down the empty street behind them.

'You bastards!' she screamed. 'Where's my son? Give him back or I'll kill you! You hear me, you fucking bastards?'

The car was too far away. Lou Ann stopped in the middle of the street and began to sob. The rain had soaked her, making her T-shirt stick to her skin. Wet hair clung to her forehead and fell in strings to her shoulders. She was shaken and dizzy from the explosion, and miserable that she hadn't gotten Jasper back. Tommy got to his feet and led her away. She leaned into him and cried. If he'd let go, he was sure she would've fallen.

They were standing in the rain, throwing eight-pointed Chinese Night Stars into tree trunks. The little weapons resembled powersaw blades with razor-sharp teeth and they crunched viciously into the bark.

'Imagine it's the lawman's forehead,' Alex hissed behind them.

Roy sighed. It was Alex's goal that his troops should be able to kill with every weapon imaginable, from their bare hands to a teapot. All they did was get high and practise killing people. Roy was getting to the point where he wouldn't have minded doing some gardening.

Behind him someone let out a shout and Roy turned to see the pink Cadillac rumbling up the road towards the camp.

'All right!' he shouted, running with the others to meet it. 'My vehicle!'

Roy scrambled down the hill. But, unlike the others who were wild with glee, the closer he got, the more unhappy he became. His pride and joy was a mess! A total fucking disaster! Bullet holes made spider webs in the windshield. One of the headlights was smashed, the grill was dented . . .

Billy Dunston jumped out of the Caddy holding the gym bag high. 'It went like a fuckin' dream, Alex!' he shouted. 'Just the way you charted it out on the blackboard with them xs and os.'

Roy walked around the car in shock. The body was dented and riddled with bullet holes. Some of the decorative chrome had been torn off. The tail lights were shattered.

The rest of the men were crowding around Alex, who now had the gym bag.

'You see?' Alex said, proudly as he unzipped the bag. 'When you men act like warriors, when you band together as one, then . . . Oh, Christ!'

For the first time Roy looked up. He saw the stunned expressions on the faces of the men as they all gazed down into the gym bag. Inside were wads of newspaper cut to resemble stacks of bills. In an instant the mood of the men went from jubilation to pure anger.

'Oh shit!' Billy Dunston groaned. 'Oh, damn!'

The others groaned and shouted as well. Only Alex, in the centre of the group, kept his cool. Roy realized he was staring straight at him.

'Oh, he's good,' Alex said softly. 'No question about that. He's so good he's got to die. And soon.'

Buddy Donovan was going to have a heart attack, Tommy thought, as he signed the forms for the rented pick-up truck. If he thought Tommy's goddamn mileage had been bad before, wait till he saw the tab on this! Outside the rental agency, he and

Lou Ann got into the pick-up and drove off. It amazed him that she'd been able to hold on to her sanity through all this chaos, especially when you considered the fact that they were no closer to Jasper now than they had been two days ago. And that brought him to another thought: it was time to plan something new.

In the pick-up Lou Ann sniffed and wiped a tear from her eye with the palm of her hand.

'How're you holding up?' Tommy asked.

'OK,' she sniffed, trying to smile. 'I have faith in you.'

'You do? Why?'

'Because I honestly think you're crazier than they are,' she said. Tommy started to frown and she could see that he wasn't taking it the way she meant it. 'What I meant was, you're good crazy and they're bad crazy. I mean, you could be one of them if you wanted, but they could never be one of you. Does that make any sense?'

'It makes sense—' Tommy began to say. He paused for a moment as a thought came. 'In fact, it gives me an idea.'

'What kind of idea?' Lou Ann asked.

'Well, like you said. I could be one of them.'

Lou Ann stared at him. 'Wait a second. Just wait a second. You're not going up to their camp. You're not going to join them!'

'Well,' Tommy said, 'I've never been much of a joiner.'

'But—' Lou Ann said.

'Sometimes you can't beat 'em,' Tommy said. '*Unless* you join 'em.'

The Wayfarer Inn was a rundown honky-tonk along the edge of the highway. The dirt parking lot was full of pot holes. A neon Coors sign glowed in the window, and most of the vehicles parked outside were pick-ups or four-wheel drives. Lou Ann steered the rented pick-up into the lot and stared over at the stranger in the seat next to her. He bore a remote resemblance to Tom Nowak, but Tom could never be as cold and vicious as this man looked. He wore a grimy green Copenhagen Snuff baseball cap, a black T-shirt and down vest, worn-out jeans and cowboy boots. There were tattoos of skulls and daggers on his arms and an icy glint in his eye.

'But what if they recognize you?' Lou Ann asked.

'The only ones who got a good look were Roy and Waycross,' Tommy said. 'I got a feeling that Waycross isn't getting around much anymore, and if Roy's there . . . Well, I'll have to improvise.'

He pushed open the door and started to get out, then turned back to Lou Ann. 'Meet me down the road at one o'clock. If you don't see me waiting, just keep on driving.'

Lou Ann nodded. Tommy gave her a wink and headed into the Wayfarer.

The bar was half-empty. A juke box in the corner played 'White Lightning' by George Jones. To Tommy's left a couple of guys were shooting pool. Tommy shuffled up to the bar and took a stool. The bartender, washing some glasses, glanced at him. He was a regular man-mountain, big as a grizzly with a bushy beard and a hard scowl. Under the apron and plaid shirt Tommy scoped out arms the size of most people's thighs. Ex-football player, he decided. And probably still in decent shape.

'What'll it be, bub?' the bartender asked.

'Shot of Four Roses and a draft,' Tommy answered in his hard voice. He tapped a quarter against the scarred wooden bar and watched the bartender draw a draft off the tap. 'So, uh, what's a fella have to do to start a little trouble around here?'

'Well, calling my mother a drunken slut would do real well for openers,' the bartender replied as he set the drinks down in front of Tommy.

'Oh, yeah?' Tommy lifted the shot glass. 'Well, your mother is' – he paused and knocked the shot back, aware that the bartender was giving him a sullen look. –'Far too nice for that.'

The bartender squinted, then smiled, and actually began to laugh. Meanwhile Tommy eyed the long rows of liquor bottles behind him.

'Uh, gimme a vodka now,' he said, grinning foolishly. 'I think I'm gonna drink me one shot of everything you got.'

The barkeep scowled at him. 'Friend, you started off pretty funny, but it sounds to me like things are gonna get awful sad.'

'You might be surprised,' Tommy said. 'I might just turn out to be one of those fellas who gets happier as he gets drunker.'

'Yeah, I heard about that type,' the bartender said. 'But I've probably served ten thousand in this joint and ain't never seen one yet.'

Tommy sat there for two hours, sipping shots, but pouring most of the liquor down the grill under the beer taps when the bartender had his back turned. Soon the bartender came over again. 'OK, Mr Happy, what'll it be *this* time?'

'It'll be a new America,' Tommy said sloppily. 'That's what it'll be. A place where a white man can stand tall for a change.'

'Right, right,' the barkeep groaned. 'You can spare me the rap. I've heard it all from those dudes in the corner.'

Tommy turned slowly. The dudes the bartender had gestured to were huddled around the pool table, smoking and drinking. They looked right. Tommy slid off his stool and strolled slowly towards them, his heart beating like a drum. As he got closer he realized that two of the pool players were the very shooters who'd stood on the hood of the Cadillac trying to kill him and Lou Ann. Now he hoped they were good and drunk, and open to a friendly game of pool. He pulled a quarter out of his pocket and placed it on the rim of the table, indicating that he had the next game. The men turned to look at him, giving him a few long, hard glares.

'Barkeep said there were a few real men over here,' Tommy said, weaving a little like a drunk. 'Now I—'

'You gonna shoot pool,' Ken-Lee shot back. 'Or you gonna talk a whole lot of dogshit?'

'I,' Tommy said, 'am going to do both.'

That got a laugh. One of the men handed Tommy a pool cue and he started to shoot, aware that Billy Dunston was squinting at him. Finally Billy lumbered drunkenly over to the table.

'Say, homeboy,' he said. 'Don't I know you?'

Tommy straightened up slowly, stared across the pool table at him and pretended to be surprised. 'Well hot damn, you're Billy Dunston, right? I remember you. About the biggest celebrity they had in all of Folsom Prison back in 1982.'

'Folsom, sure,' Billy grinned and appeared to relax. 'And what's your name, partner?'

'Will Van Syke,' Tommy said.

'What'd they get you for?' Ken-Lee asked.

'Three felonies,' Tommy said, bending over the table to make another shot. 'Three big F's. Assault with intent, B and E, and having carnal knowledge of a motor vehicle.'

The guys laughed at that one. Tommy straightened up and grinned at them. 'Hey, what can I say? That little Corvette was just beggin' for it!'

After months of listening to humourless Alex, the Birthright boys appeared primed for some comedy. They laughed and threw around a few high-fives.

'We need this dude,' Darrell said, slapping Tommy on the back, causing him to miss his shot and lose his turn. Tommy backed away from the table and leaned on his pool cue. He noticed that Ken-Lee had sidled up to him and was rolling up the sleeve of his shirt to reveal a crudely made tattoo.

'Read my bicep,' he said, his breath heavy with rye.

'Death before dishonour,' Tommy read.

'Words I live by,' Ken-Lee announced. 'Carved 'em in with a piece of copper wire. Thing is, there's a dude around here who dishonoured us. You hear? Dishonoured us!'

'Uh, who's that?' Tommy asked, swallowing.

'Skip tracer, dude,' Darrel said. 'Ripped off our leader. Killed one of our baddest men.'

Tommy set his jaw and put a glint in his eye. 'Then he's got to go down.'

'Damn straight,' grunted Billy.

'Righteous,' added Darrel.

'An eye for an eye,' said Ken-Lee,

'No, man,' Tommy told them. 'A head for an eye.'

They loved it. It fit right into their deranged macho inferiority complexes. Tommy started to relax. The smoky hours passed. They played more pool, drank more booze and talked more horseshit. But intermixed were bits and pieces of the story of how they'd tried to kill Tommy and Lou Ann at the car wash. They also invited Tommy to come up to the Birthright camp the following day and meet Alex. After a while Billy Dunston announced he had to go take a leak.

'I'll go with you,' Darrell said.

'Me too,' said Ken-Lee.

Jesus, like a bunch of girls at a dance, Tommy thought. Then he noticed they were all looking at him.

'Oh, I'm coming,' he said, quickly laying down his stick.

The men's room was a small, foul-smelling room, with more toilet paper on the floor than anywhere else. There were only two urinals and Billy and Ken-Lee took them. Tommy bent over the sink and splashed some water on to his face. Darrell had backed up against the men's room door and was snorting some crystal meth off his fingernail.

'Want some?' he asked Tommy.

'No, thanks,' Tommy said. 'I'm kinda high on life.'

The guys took it as a joke. Tommy took the opportunity to talk a little more about the incident at the car wash.

'Now, you were saying you had the vehicle trapped inside a car wash and you couldn't finish the dude off?' he said.

Ken-Lee gave him a look. 'Aw, maybe we're talking too much.'

'Fuck that,' Darrell said. 'He's one of us.'

'Then let him try dealin' with the fuckin' Nowak dude,' Billy said from the urinal. He pulled a cigarette from between his lips and gestured at Tommy. 'You can't believe how pissed I am. I mean, I've been busted down to fuckin' guard duty with that jerk-off Roy. And I still swear we did everything possible to waste that fuck. You implying we didn't?'

'I don't know,' Tommy said, watching where Billy's hand and cigarette went after he finished talking. 'But you'd be a whole lot more convincing if you weren't pissing on your cigarette.'

The boys looked up and broke out laughing. The high-fives started flying again, they slapped each other on the back and roared with laughter. Even Billy Dunston had tears in his eyes from laughing so hard. He kept pointing at Tommy and saying, 'This fuckin' dude . . . this *fuckin'* dude . . .' But he always choked on laughter before he could finish the sentence. After a while they caught their breaths.

'Let's clear outta here,' Ken-Lee said, yawning. He nodded to Tommy. 'We'll talk more tomorrow, OK? Up at the camp.'

'Yeah,' Tommy said. 'Sure.'

He made some excuse about having to settle his tab with the bartender and waited until they'd left. Then he went out and walked toward the spot where he told Lou Ann to pick him up. The cold crisp air was almost overpowering after the hours of smoke and booze he'd ingested, and the stars seemed to shimmer twice as much as usual in the midnight blue sky. He was light-headed and dizzy. Even while trying not to drink he'd managed to consume nearly a month's supply of bourbon and beer.

Right on time Lou Ann came down the highway and stopped for him. Tommy climbed uncertainly into the cab and slammed the door.

'OK, let's get the hell out of here,' he groaned.

'Oh boy, it sure smells like you had a good time,' Lou Ann said.

Tommy rubbed his face in his hands. 'You're telling me. Feels like I've been in that bar for six months.'

'So? Did you meet them?'

'Oh, yeah,' Tommy sighed. 'I met them.'

'Did they tell you where the camp is?' Lou Ann asked eagerly.

'Sure did,' Tommy said, staring at the white lines of the highway as they slid under the headlights. 'In fact, I'm going up there tomorrow.'

'I'm coming with you,' Lou Ann said.

'Uh, we'll talk about it in the morning,' Tommy said wearily. He was too tired and tipsy to argue with her now.

'And I want you to give me one of your guns,' Lou Ann added.

'No,' Tommy said flatly. 'I have a very firm policy on gun control. Any time there's a gun nearby, I want to be the one who controls it.'

'Change your policy,' Lou Ann said.

Tommy closed his eyes and pressed his fingers against his eyeballs. This whole thing was going too far. 'Look, Lou Ann. I've already broken every rule in the book for you. I've practically written new books just so I could break new rules! Now how far do you want me to go?'

'All the way,' Lou Ann replied.

11

Mistrustful of the motels in the area after the experience at World O' Wonders, they spent the night in the pick-up, parked up a dirt logging road off the highway. In the morning they woke up stiff and groggy and climbed down through the trees to a spring-fed stream where they threw cold water on their faces. Later, back in the pick-up, Tommy loaded his .22 and Roy's .45. Lou Ann watched quietly. They shared a certain grim camaraderie in facing the difficult task that lay ahead.

'Don't mean to be macho,' Tommy said, handing her the .22.

'But girls always do the cooking and get the smaller calibres,' Lou Ann said, accepting the pistol.

'Sure you know how to use it?' Tommy asked.

'Yes, Roy taught me,' she said, flicking the safety on and off. 'He thought it would make us closer if we could go shooting together.'

'The family that shoots together, huh?' Tommy said.

'Nothing decent rhymes with it,' Lou Ann said. 'I promise you.'

They rode up the highway and turned off at a sign that said MARIPOSA – 4 Miles. The new road was dirt. Up ahead it turned rutted and narrow as it wound upwards through the dense pine and fir forest towards the foothills.

'You may have to duck down,' Tommy said, switching the pick-up into four-wheel drive.

They drove a few more miles and saw a small white guard post in the distance. The pink Cadillac was parked next to it.

'Oh, man,' Tommy groaned. 'I can't get away from that car.'

'Time to duck,' Lou Ann said, crouching below the glove compartment. 'Seems like I've been spending an awful lot of time in this position.'

'Great for the back, I hear,' Tommy quipped.

The pick-up bounced and scooted up the road. As they approached the guard house, Roy stepped out carrying Murray's old carbine. He raised his hand for the pick-up to stop.

'You won't believe who's in the guard house,' Tommy whispered out of the side of his mouth as he pulled his cap low over his eyes.

'All right,' Roy shouted. 'Hold it right there.' Not suspecting that anything was out of order, he walked around to the driver's side of the pick-up, holding the carbine low by his side. Tommy rolled down the pick-up's window and stuck the .45 in Roy's face.

'Hello, Roy,' Tommy said, tipping up his cap. 'We've come for the baby.'

Lou Ann stuck her head up. The look on her husband's face was one of total shock. He stared intently at the gun in Tommy's hand.

'That's mine,' Roy said.

'Gee, I'm sorry, Roy,' Tommy replied. 'But is it OK that I've borrowed it for a while?'

'God, first you take my car,' Roy sulked. 'Then my wife and now my gun.'

'Are you sure about the order of those things?' Tommy asked.

Instead of answering, Roy started to laugh. He was laughing so hard he was practically doubled over. Tommy kept the gun on him in case it was a ruse.

'What's so funny, Roy?' Lou Ann asked.

'Me,' Roy gasped, straightening up. 'Jesus Christ, I get busted all the way down to guard duty and I still manage to fuck that up. I swear, ever since I was sixteen years old I never did anything right.'

'Why don't you start now?' Tommy asked seriously. 'Help us get the kid.'

Roy looked around and stepped closer to the pick-up. 'What's your plan?'

'Well, plan A is we leave the pick-up here and I go up there as Will Van Slyke, meet Alex, and keep everyone distracted while you and Lou Ann take off with the baby,' Tommy said.

'What's plan B?' Lou Ann asked.

'All hell breaks loose,' Tommy replied.

Roy went back to the guard post to get the keys for the

Caddy. Then all three of them walked over to the bullet-riddled car.

'So who's drivin' now?' Roy asked glumly.

Tommy smiled back at him. 'My treat.'

Lou Ann started to get in the front, but Tommy cleared his throat. 'The back?' she asked.

'The floor in the back, I'm afraid,' Tommy said.

Lou Ann rolled her eyes and climbed in. 'Just once I'd like to sit in a car seat again.'

'With any kind of luck you will,' Tommy said, getting in next to Roy.

They rode up the bumpy craggy trail, past the towering evergreens and huge boulders toward the next guard post. The morning sun filtered through the trees, throwing ornate patterns on the forest greenery. A hawk circled high above.

'Billy Dunston's up there,' Roy said. 'He got busted down to guard duty like me, only I think he's a lot more sore about it.'

'So I heard,' Tommy said. 'But tell me, Roy. Why two guard posts?'

'This one's where Alex keeps the plastic explosives,' Roy said. 'He don't want to keep 'em in the camp lest there's an accident and we all get blown to kingdom come.'

The second guard post was a toolshed. As the Caddy approached, Billy Dunston emerged carrying a rifle and a frown. He looked pretty hung over.

'I got a visitor here,' Roy said, pulling the Caddy over.

'I can see that,' Billy snapped. 'Who the hell gave you permission to leave your damn post?'

Tommy vaulted over the side of the car and faced Billy.

'Hey, come on, Billy,' he said. 'Let's not—'

'You stay out of this, Will,' Billy replied. He started to turn back to Roy, then stopped and stared at Tommy as if in the sunlight something suddenly became clear to him. 'Hey, wait a second. I don't know you from Folsom. I know you from—'

Before he could finish, Tommy smacked him hard into the tool shed, banging his head against the doorframe.

'The car wash,' Tommy finished the sentence for him as Billy went down, unconscious.

'Nice of you to refresh his memory,' Lou Ann said from the backseat.

Tommy got back into the Caddy and they drove the rest of the way up to the camp. No one was around, but they could hear gunfire coming from the target range. Roy stopped the car and pointed to a small shack up the hill.

'That's where Jasper is,' he whispered.

'Alone?' Tommy asked.

'Naw, Darrell's watching him.'

'Good, wait here,' Tommy said, hopping out of the car. He leaned over the side and touched Lou Ann's shoulder. 'Come on.'

Lou Ann got out and they headed for the small shack. Tommy noticed that there was an open window in the back.

'Think you could crawl through that window and grab Jasper while I keep Darrell occupied?' he asked in a low voice.

'I'm sure willing to try,' Lou Ann whispered back.

Tommy went up to the front door. Darrell was sitting inside, flipping through a copy of *Soap Opera Digest*. Behind him Tommy saw the glint of sunlight on a row of glass cases. Rifle cases, he guessed from the shape of them. There was a wicker basinet in there too, no doubt where Jasper was currently residing. Tommy stepped up to the door and knocked. Inside Darrell looked up.

'Will Van Slyke!' he said with a grin and came to the door.

'Yo, Darrell,' Tommy said in his Van Slyke voice.

'So how you doin', bud?' Darrell asked, opening the door. 'Man, you were funnier'n hell last night. We could use a few more laughs around here.'

Behind Darrell, Tommy could see Lou Ann sliding through the back window. He put his arm around Darrell's shoulder and led him a few steps away from the doorway.

'Yeah,' Tommy said. 'More laughs. But Darrell, I was just thinkin'. If we get rid of all the Jews and Blacks, man, who's gonna be our comedians?'

Darrell pondered the question as seriously as if someone had asked him about the meaning of life. Meanwhile, out of the corner of Tommy's eye he watched Lou Ann scoop up Jasper in her arms.

'Well,' Darrell said. 'We still got David Letterman.'

'Yeah,' Tommy said, grimly. 'David Letterman.'

'Well, damn,' Darrell said. 'We can't have everything. I mean—'

In the shack behind them a floorboard creaked. As Darrell whirled around, Tommy pulled out the .45 and whacked him on the back of the head. Darrell's knees buckled, but Tommy caught him and dragged him back into the shack.

'God, I'm sorry,' Lou Ann whispered. 'I should've seen that loose board.'

'Don't sweat it,' Tommy whispered back as he propped Darrell back in his seat. 'Let's just get the hell out of here.'

They slipped out of the shack and cut back behind it, staying low, keeping between the outbuildings and the forest as they made their way down the hill towards the Cadillac. Suddenly Tommy saw Billy Dunston staggering up the road from the guard house.

'Code red!' Billy shouted. 'Code fuckin' red!'

Tommy grabbed Lou Ann and pulled her behind a tree. Hearing Billy's shouts, the Birthright boys started to pour out of the buildings with guns drawn.

'Well, so much for plan A,' Tommy whispered.

Lou Ann cuddled Jasper, holding him tightly.

'I don't care what happens,' she whispered. 'I won't let him go again.'

Tommy pressed his finger to his lips. The Birthright boys were spreading out to search for them. They blocked the trail to the Cadillac and back beyond it to the pick-up. The only way out now was to head back across the camp and down the sloping wooded hills leading to the valley.

'Come on,' Tommy whispered, rising. They made their way around the back of the buildings, pausing behind the largest of them, the one Tommy had heard the shots coming from earlier. There was an open doorway, but Tommy wasn't interested in exploring. The trees were just a few dozen yards away, and he knew that if they could get to them they had a chance of making it out of this mess alive.

Suddenly one of the Birthright boys came huffing around a corner. Tommy pushed Lou Ann inside the doorway.

It was dark inside. They stood silently in the shadows, waiting for their eyes to adjust. A strange sight began to take shape before them. It looked like they'd stepped into the backstage area of a theatre. It made no sense at all, and yet the set looked like some kind of town complete with a bank, post office and drug store. But why the armoured car? And why cut-out figures with bales of hay behind them? The answer suddenly hit Tommy.

'Jesus,' he hissed. 'It's a target range.'

Suddenly there were footsteps. Tommy kept Lou Ann low. It sounded like someone was singing, and the voice was familiar.

'Hello, young lovers wherever you are . . .' the voice sang. Tommy knew it was Alex. Behind him some of the others were yelling and laughing. They must've thought this was a treat, tracking down the quarry and killing it right there in their own camp.

Tommy and Lou Ann hid behind the bank. Jasper was squirming and Lou Ann kept her hand over the baby's mouth to muffle his cries. The Birthright was in the target range now. Tommy looked back at the doorway he and Lou Ann had come through. The sunlight glared in from outside. That was their only escape, but he knew as soon as they were in the doorway they'd be seen. He had to divert the others.

'Listen,' he whispered to Lou Ann. 'As soon as I squeeze off shot one, you head for that door, take off through the woods and don't look back. If you think you can make it to the pick-up, take it.'

Lou Ann stared at him, feeling the impact of his words. Without a car he had no way of escape. Tommy patted her shoulder.

'It'll be all right,' he whispered. 'Now get ready.'

He knew he was going to draw a lot of fire and he wanted to get as far away from Lou Ann and the baby as possible. He crawled behind a figure of a policeman off to the right and watched as the Birthright boys crept into the target range.

'Oh, tracer,' Alex called, taunting him. 'Time to come out and—'

Tommy slid the .45 under the policeman's make-believe gun and squeezed off a single shot. He heard someone grunt, then a thud as a body hit the floor. As a fusillade of lead tore into the policeman target Tommy dove to the right and rolled out of the way. He was behind the bank again. Hopefully Lou Ann had made it out of the target range and was heading through the woods. The Birthright boys were still throwing everything they had at the cop target. Roy was in there with them, but Tommy didn't have time to figure out whose side he was on now. He drew a bead on another one and fired through bars of the teller's cage. Another Birthright boy dropped with a thud as Tommy rolled out of the way of more bullets.

Suddenly there was a shout from outside. 'Got her!' Tommy recognized Billy Dunston's voice.

The shooting stopped. A moment later Bill Dunston dragged Lou Ann into the target range. She was still clutching Jasper.

'Drop your weapon, tracer,' Alex said, aiming his gun at Lou Ann. 'Right now, or she goes down.'

Reluctantly, Tommy slid his gun across the floor.

'OK,' Alex said. 'Now come out, nicely.'

Tommy came out slowly from behind the backdrop. Alex came towards him, his gun pointed at Tommy's face. Roy and the others stood in the backround. Billy was holding Lou Ann tight. She was shaking, visibly terrified.

'Fuck up the dude's face, Alex,' Billy Dunston urged Alex. 'Fuck it up good!'

'Ease up, Billy,' Alex said, keeping his gun on Tommy. 'You'll have your fun in just a minute.'

The leader of the Birthright came towards Tommy with a fascinated look on his face, as if he was meeting an extraterrestrial for the first time.

'How'd you manage to sneak past Roy?' Alex asked.

Tommy glanced at Roy and smirked. 'People've been sneaking past Roy all his life. You know that.'

Alex chuckled. 'None of this had to happen, you know. If you had just stayed out of it.'

Suddenly Lou Ann burst out of Billy's grasp and ran to Tommy, clutching him tearfully as she fumbled to hold up Jasper. Alex didn't move. He kept his gun aimed at Tommy.

'See,' he said. 'If I go back to prison I die there. And you two can put me there and slam the door for ever. So you tell me: what choice do I have?'

Lou Ann continued to cling to Tommy, sobbing hysterically. He wanted to tell her that this really wasn't the right time, but then he felt something hard and cold press against his back. The .22! He reached behind with his left hand and took it.

Meanwhile, Alex had turned to his men. 'Take 'em out into the woods and—'

Tommy hit him with an uppercut, grabbed him around the neck and pressed the .22 to the side of his head. The Birthright boys instantly raised their guns.

'Nobody shoot!' Alex gasped, staring at Billy. 'You idiot! Didn't you frisk her?'

'But she's a female,' Billy replied, biting his lip.

Tommy pulled Alex back, keeping the gun pressed tightly against his head. Alex was trembling like a newborn baby chick. The rest of the Birthright watched helplessly.

'Now listen, boys,' Tommy said. 'Here's the programme. We all walk down to the Cadillac together. We all leave. We all live. I'll set you free a few miles down the highway. OK?'

The Birthright boys didn't seem particularly thrilled by the idea. At least, they still had their guns aimed at him.

'Hold your fire,' Alex ordered. 'I'm going down the hill with these people.'

Slowly, and with excruciating care, Tommy started to back through Silhouette City, holding Alex tightly. Lou Ann stayed close to him. The gang followed, looking dazed and confused. Suddenly Lou Ann backed into a target, knocking it over. She and Tommy both jumped and stared down at it, stunned. There was a photo of *her face* taped to the target, riddled with bullet holes.

Out of the corner of his eye, Tommy saw Billy Dunston raise his gun, as if to pick him off. Tommy straightened up and pressed the barrel of the .22 against Alex's forehead. He moved his lips near Alex's ear.

'If they're gonna start shooting, Alex, you might as well tell me. Do you want to be an organ donor?'

'OK, drop your weapons,' Alex ordered.

With great reluctance, the gang dropped their guns. Tommy, Lou Ann and Alex backed through the doorway into the sunlight outside. They squinted in the sudden brightness. The rest of the Birthright boys followed, squinting as well. Still holding Alex tightly Tommy began to walk backwards towards the Cadillac. For once in his life it was a beautiful sight.

The gang followed, but as Lou Ann and Tommy neared the car, Tommy suddenly pointed the gun at them. 'OK, stop there. Don't come any closer.'

The gang stopped. Lou Ann and Jasper got in the car. Tommy let go of Alex and nudged him with the gun. 'All right, get in.'

But Alex didn't move. He glanced back at his men and seemed to be smiling.

'I said get in,' Tommy ordered.

'They'll never let you out alive,' Alex said, ignoring him. 'They're not that fucking dumb.'

'I disagree,' Tommy said, still aiming the gun at Alex. He had to admit the leader of the Birthright had balls. Not only was he refusing to get in the Cadillac and daring Tommy to shoot him, but now he was backing up the hill towards the others. The trouble was, he was right. They both knew Tommy couldn't shoot an unarmed man.

'You ought to kill me in cold blood,' Alex taunted him. ' Really. You won't be safe until I'm dead. You know you want to pull the trigger. I would.'

Still holding the gun on Alex, Tommy got into the Cadillac. He turned the key in the ignition and floored it.

The gang scattered. Tommy figured they'd have to get back up to the camp for their guns and by then he and Lou Ann would be out of reach. The Caddy was flying down the logging road as fast as Tommy could go without losing control. Tommy fought the steering wheel, trying to keep the big car on the narrow trail.

As they approached an intersection of another logging road, Tommy thought he heard something. No, it couldn't be!

Tommy couldn't believe his eyes. Coming down the other road was a Jeep with Alex, Billy and Darrell in it. They must've had it stashed in the woods for emergencies. Bullets shot past his ears. The Caddy's whole windshield shattered, showering him with splintered E-Z-eye glass.

'Down!' Tommy shouted, pushing Lou Ann to the floor as the Cadillac bounced and careened down the trail, smashing through branches, with the Jeep thirty feet behind, guns blaring in a roar. Fighting the steering wheel with one hand, Tommy managed to get off a few shots with the .45. He forced Alex to swerve up on two wheels. Someone tumbled out of the Jeep, but Tommy didn't have time to figure out who as the Caddy itself caught a rut and suddenly pulled hard to the right. Tommy yanked the steering wheel, but it was too late. The Cadillac smashed into a small tree, sending branches, pine needles and pine cones flying everywhere.

Tommy opened his eyes. The Caddy was still rolling, a few pine branches stuck in the grill. Lou Ann, with Jasper still in her arms, was trying to fight her way out from under the small branches that had landed in the passenger seat. A bullet flew through the windshield frame and another took out the rear-view mirror. Tommy turned around and exchanged fire.

Suddenly the Caddy's engine sputtered. Steam was starting to hiss out from under the hood. Tommy felt the car losing power. Meanwhile the Jeep was pulling alongside them, Alex and Billy both leaning towards them with MAC-10s in their hands. Tommy looked ahead and saw the second guardpost coming up on the left. He had once last chance. At the last possible second he yanked the steering wheel left, smashing into the side of the Jeep. Alex grabbed the wheel, but before he could regain control, the Jeep veered out of control, crashing into the guard house.

Ka-boom! The explosion was tremendous as the Jeep and the guardhouse went up in a ball of flame, a hundred feet high. Burning debris shot out in every direction, and a great cloud of black smoke rose into the air. Fifty yards down the road the Cadillac rolled to a stop. Lou Ann finally managed to scramble off the floor of the car. She and Tommy watched the burning remnants of the Jeep and shack. Suddenly, except for the crackles and pops of the flames, everything was silent. Thanks for the plastic explosives, Tommy thought.

At the very top of the road, the remaining members of the Birthright began to appear, looking down at the charred remains of their fearless leader. Tommy could just make out Roy, Darrell and the others, their faces etched with bewilderment as they realized Alex was gone, and with it the whole Birthright movement. The only angry face appeared to be Darrell's. He started to lift a rifle and aim.

Tommy turned the key in the ignition. The Cadillac coughed and sputtered.

Lou Ann looked at him in horror and covered Jasper's head.

A shot smashed into the dashboard between Tommy and Lou Ann, disintegrating the radio. Tommy cranked the ignition key. Lou Ann ducked lower. Darrell started to aim again. He was just about to pull the trigger when Roy hit him sideways with a crossbody block.

The Caddy's engine started.

Tommy waved and took off for the highway.

They drove through the huge Redwoods of Placer Valley, the great cinnamon-red trunks rising majestically towards the heavens. The passengers in every car they passed stared at them. The Caddy's grill was smashed and still carried the remains of the tree they'd hit. The windshield was gone, the body dented, scraped and bullet riddled. Tommy was still picking pine needles out of his hair. Next to him, Lou Ann hugged Jasper.

'How're you feeling?' Tommy asked.

'I feel,' Lou Ann began with a sigh. 'I feel like I've just had this baby. Like I just gave birth.'

Tommy smiled. It must have been an apt description, but frankly, *he* felt hungry.

'But what now?' Lou Ann asked.

'Well, right now you and I are both outlaws,' Tommy said. 'So either we turn into stone criminals, and I'm talking bank jobs, blackmail, fencing stolen treasures from the Orient and so on, or we go back to Sacramento and run the whole story past the district attorney, and straighten things out together.'

'You really think we can work it out?' Lou Ann asked.

'It'll take some work,' Tommy said. 'But I think we can do it. And if something goes wrong – if they make us run – we'll just run a whole lot faster than them.'

They rode on for a while. Lou Ann waved happily at everyone who gaped at the car.

'You know,' she said. 'I hope the case gets cleared up quickly so that we can set up our new skip-chaser agency.'

'Now wait a second,' Tommy laughed. 'First of all, I've told you a million times, it's skip *tracer*.'

'I don't know,' Lou Ann said. 'Seems like an equal mix of tracing and chasing to me. Anyway we could do TV commercials.

143

You in that gold blazer and me in my slinky red dress.'

'Sure,' Tommy said. 'Like, "Hi, we're Nowak and McGuinn. And we'd like to be your fugitive people." '

Lou Ann turned around and saw her red dress on the floor in front of the rear seat. She picked it up and brushed the pine needles off.

'You think they'll make me give it back?' she asked.

'Honey,' Tommy said, sliding his arm around her shoulders. 'As far as I'm concerned, they don't know *anything* about the money you used to buy that dress. Get my drift? And if there's *any* justice in this world at *all*, you'll never have to give it back.'